## SEND IN TH

"News?" asked President Proctor.
"Not direct."
The President turned away. Then Leonard Meyer's eyes told him there was more.
"Well?" he asked.
"This man Ross who the hijackers have. You know, Mr Ordinary."
The President had absorbed the briefings well. "Yes. Personal animosity. Broke the elementary rule in dealing with hijackers not to antagonise them . . ." He began sorting through the papers to find a note.
"He's more than that, Mr President."
"What is he?" After the tension of his meeting with Muntwick the President began to laugh skittishly. "The Pope in disguise, the Party Treasurer absconding with the funds . . .?"
Meyer's voice held no amusement. He managed to keep it even but it was still imbued with the tension he felt.
"Mr President," he said, "he knows about Operation Whiphand."

**Also by the same author, and available in Coronet Books:**

The Sleeper

# Send in the Lions

---

## Eric Clark

CORONET BOOKS
Hodder and Stoughton

First published in Great Britain 1981
by Hodder and Stoughton Ltd

*Coronet edition 1982*

**British Library C.I.P.**

Clark, Eric, 1937–
Send in the lions.
I. Title
823'.914[F] PR6053.L295

ISBN 0 340 284390

---

*The characters and situations in this book are entirely imaginary and bear no relation to any real person or actual happening*



Printed and bound in Great Britain for Hodder and Stoughton Paperbacks, a division of Hodder and Stoughton Ltd., Mill Road, Dunton Green, Sevenoaks, Kent (Editorial Office: 47 Bedford Square, London, WC1 3DP) by Richard Clay (The Chaucer Press) Ltd., Bungay, Suffolk

For my mother

## Acknowledgments

Many people have helped me in researching the background to this book and in particular I would like to record my thanks to:

Iann Barron of Inmos
British Airways
Simon Clarke
Tony Collins and B. P. Barnett Crossbows
D.
Catherine Dodds
Dr Vivian Gartside
Stanley Gibbons Ltd.
Raymond Hawkey
Dennis Kenyon and Spooner Aviation
Dr A. G. Marshall
Dr R. M. Needham, of the Computer Laboratory of the University of Cambridge
Len Tiller and Interoute
And Monks of the Cistercian Order.

'Dogs in a kennel snarl at each other;
but when a wolf comes along, they become allies.'

*The Talmud*

# Prologue

## Northern Spain, early January, 1985

The monks were burying their departed Brother.

For most of one day and all of one night the body had lain near the high altar of the austere Gothic church, the cross and burning Paschal candle at its foot.

Not once had it been left alone. A constant stream of monks in their white Cistercian cowls had knelt to pray or to chant their psalms.

Now it was the afternoon of the day after the death and the burial service was entering the final commendation and salutation. The body, uncoffined, was being sprinkled with holy water as the monks' voices rose:

*"He who believes in Me, as the Scripture has said, 'Out of his heart shall flow rivers of living water', and I shall raise him up on the last day . . ."*

A hundred yards away, in another austere building that made up the fourth side of the monastery's cloisters, nine other men, none of them monks, were grouped together in a first-floor room.

There was no sound from the church this far away; only the noise of the men's voices as they argued, and the flurries of rain against the single arched window.

There was a man at the window, looking out on to the gently wooded slope down into the valley and, beyond, the foothills of the mountains.

Perhaps fifty yards away he could see the low stone walls of the community's cemetery with its rows of stark black crosses and the freshly dug grave standing waiting with its barrow of earth beside.

As he stared down, the bells began – a special sound reserved for a dead man: two bells sounding together; the larger one being rung, the smaller one being tolled. The procession to the cemetery had begun.

The man, who was Irish and named Michael O'Dare Flynn, shuddered in fear for his own death. There was a sudden silence in the room behind him, and he turned. The room, like the rest of the monastery, was spartan. The walls were whitewashed stone, broken only by a wooden crucifix and some small framed prayers and quotations. It was furnished with plain wooden chairs and a large refectory table.

One doorway led to a passageway and the cubicled dormitory the men had shared for the previous three nights, the only outsiders at the monastery. Another opened on to a curving stone staircase to ground floor rooms, one of which, in turn, contained the entrance to the enclosure of the monastery proper.

Seven of the men in the room were seated around the table which, incongruously for such a place, was covered in papers, ashtrays, glasses and two open bottles of Soberano brandy. Normally it was not a risk the men would have taken. But this afternoon they knew they were safe from visit.

The eighth man, Montoya, the Basque, was adding logs to the fire. The room was already hot, another reason Flynn had moved nearer the window.

The Irishman was only partially conscious of the talk inside the room which was again animated and passionate after the brief silence. The Arab, Hassan, was leading today's discussions. He was having difficulty keeping peace between the German, Greif, and the Ukrainian, Titov.

This was the second time the men had used the monastery for their meeting. Flynn did not doubt they would use it again.

Ostensibly they were all in retreat, refreshing themselves spiritually. But when they were alone, in the dormitory or this room, they talked not of God, but of revolution and destruction and murder.

The German was waving a newspaper now. Flynn did not need to listen to what the man was saying. The newspaper, like others heaped on the table, was six days old. The main story was the signing of the Anti-Terrorist Convention in Geneva.

For the first time the major powers had reached some measure of accord – not easy because one country's terrorist had always been someone else's freedom fighter.

But the fast escalation and geographical spread of terrorism in the previous two years had forced all countries to the conference table. Even Libya, for long the terrorist's best friend, had signed the Convention – forced to do so because of its need of Western technology.

And, just as dramatically, so too had the Soviet Union, after witnessing growing outside help and support for internal dissident groups and a series of violent incidents.

Which was why the meeting was producing such passion and why Greif and his supporters were arguing for action to show the world their capabilities remained real.

Flynn turned back to the window. Below, the procession was emerging into the rain: the holy water, the candle, the cross carried before the body, the abbot following and behind, the monks, the most senior first, leather sandalled feet taking the steps into the garden and beyond that into the cemetery.

The bells had stopped now and the last part of the procession was in silence.

The Irishman lifted his eyes, beyond the cemetery. Nothing moved. It *was* a good site. Ideal for their purposes, isolated, not far from the border and the old smuggling tracks, and surrounded by woodland in which colleagues could watch for strangers.

In the silence he half heard the Arab behind him exhorting the others not to fight each other. But he disregarded the discussion: the real guts of the meeting were over. A majority had already decided – action, yes, but not yet. They would all disperse tomorrow. This was talk for its own sake.

And the service drew him. Was it because he had been brought up as a Catholic; did it ever totally lose its hold? Or was it death itself?

The body, still uncoffined, face uncovered, was being lowered into the grave, head towards the east and the rising sun.

The abbot sprinkled soil into the grave, and then the monks began shovelling earth, black and heavy from the rain.

The wind caught the rain and drove it through the partially open window, making the Irishman move his head instinctively. As he did, something attracted his eye, far beyond the cemetery, down the slope where the trees began.

It was so unexpected that it took him several seconds to absorb what he had seen – a man darting from one tree to another.

He waited a further minute. There was nothing else, but there was no need.

He still had his glass in his hand and he walked to the table and carefully set it down before talking to the Basque.

"You have guards posted?" he asked. His voice was matter of fact but his fingertips were tingling. Montoya nodded, surprised by the question.

"Would one of them dart across a clearing, his face turned this way?"

Three men made for the window at once. The Irishman's voice stopped them. "For God's sake don't go showing them we know. That's all we've got."

"Someone sold us out." The German's voice was full of hurt.

"Not our men."

"For God's sake, let's just concentrate on getting out."

Even during the brief exchange, the men had been grabbing their pistols, concealed in a case in the corner.

"I see one. Now another. They're moving in slowly." The speaker was the Frenchman, Séverine, the one lookout.

In the brief silence, a line of psalm entered the room: *"Fresh and green are the pastures where he gives me repose."*

"Why are they waiting?"

There was a pause and then Flynn realised the answer.

"The funeral," he said. "They're waiting for the funeral to end. They can hear it just as we can."

He began to laugh. "They're all good Catholics. Oh, bless religion."

Voices merged in a rapid council of war. Ideas came quickly: escape through the church and out of the east door where there was only a short sprint to farm buildings . . . go along the south cloister, past the library, through wash houses and along the orchard wall . . . stay and fight it out.

Urgency forced the decision. The men left and took the staircase in single file. The Irishman was last – he had paused to check the window. The burial service continued, the monks oblivious to what was now happening all around them.

Downstairs the heavy wood and metal door to the enclosure slid open silently. The south cloister was in half-darkness despite the hour, with only pools of light from slit windows picked out on the marble floor.

As if by instinct, the men divided into four groups, three of two, one of three. The first two, the Basque and the Arab, went first. They had decided on the church and the east door.

The German and the Frenchman followed, vanishing as they turned towards the library. The Ukrainian and the Argentinian, Martinez, had waited; now they followed, planning to take the exit into the orchard.

Flynn, the Italian, Quaroni, and the American, Peters, all planned to attempt the quickest route – along the cloister, and out the first exit, the one the monks had taken. Crouched, they would then skirt the cemetery wall, using it as cover, before making a dash for outbuildings and then the trees.

They had almost reached the exit when the American, in the lead, stopped suddenly, his hand raised. "They're coming back," he whispered.

"Retreat. Hide. Let them pass," said Flynn.

They retraced their steps, but had barely reached the cloister when there was a crash from the Guest House – the huge entrance door being swung open.

"They're inside!"

Flynn peered in the darkness, raising his pistol ready. Would the civil guard open fire in a monastery? A crazy question. They would – without hesitation.

Then he remembered. The cowls. There were always a few spare ones hanging in a corridor off the cloister. He led the way, his decisiveness making the others follow.

He had been right. The men pulled cowls over their clothes.

As the silent procession passed, the three men slipped out and joined it. Inside the church he could see the monks staring in puzzlement as the abbot gave the final prayer.

There was the sound of gunfire, first from outside, and then as though it had echoed inside the monastery building.

Several monks raised their heads, but the abbot appeared not to have heard:

*"May the blood of your Son, the price of his redemption keep far from him the flames of hell. Through the same Christ our Lord."*

There was silence for many moments and then the monks began to file away. Flynn, Quaroni and Peters joined them, heads down, weapons concealed but ready.

The Irishman and Peters turned off as soon as they could, melting into a corridor. They could no longer see the Italian.

There were civil guards outside, but the two men walked unhurriedly, heads still bowed. The Irishman judged they would have to run soon – the fact they were heading away from the monastery would make them suspect.

But the shout to stop came sooner than he had thought. He turned and saw a guard pointing towards his feet – the guard had spotted that he wore shoes and not sandals over white socks.

Peters was already running and Flynn fired off two quick shots and followed him, slithering on the wet grass and trying to throw off the cowl as he ran.

The hillside was alive with the noise of shooting now and there were echoes from inside the building they had left behind.

Flynn could not know but, of the seven behind, one was already dead, two were trapped in the Chapter House, one was lying unconscious in the Scriptorium, another was pinned down unable to move in the corner of the church, and the final two were being led violently from an outbuilding.

Flynn and Peters both had their cowls off now and, almost impossibly, had reached the trees. The Irishman began to feel elation and then he saw Peters fall, hit by a bullet. He froze on the wet ground until the soldier who had fired the shot was over the body and then Flynn fired three times.

The soldier was dead when Flynn reached him, his face and chest both seeping blood. Peters was alive, but too badly injured to move. The Irishman shot him in the side of the head, averting his eyes.

Then he rose and began running, darting from tree to tree. The mist enveloped him and he thought he was clear. He stopped, his lungs gasping. The shooting had fallen away and there was a great stillness.

He began to move again, slowly now, more cautiously. Two civil guards, their weapons raised, appeared out of the mist in front of him.

He froze for a moment and then began to raise his own pistol.

From high up on the hill behind him the big bell began tolling again.

It was the last sound the Irishman heard before the rifle butt crashed on his skull from behind, but as he collapsed into the cold, wet grass he thought he heard in the moment before he lost consciousness the chant of the monks . . .

*"I was punished, I was punished by the Lord, but not doomed to die."*

# I

## Sunday, 24 March 1985

Karen Huisman opened the special Concorde menu, pleased to have something mundane to occupy her. Even so, she was conscious of the glances of the man across the aisle. She was, she knew, a woman who attracted attention. She was almost six feet tall, had a mass of black hair, swept high in curls, and a pale face with large dark eyes and high cheekbones.

The menu, in a dark blue cover decorated with a gold crown, was meant to reflect the luxuriousness of the supersonic flight. And, despite the cramped space compared with larger aircraft, Concorde flying had become more special in the nine years since the first transatlantic service simply because air travel generally had become ever more ordinary and devoid of frills. That was the reason why today's passengers were prepared to pay substantially more than the normal first-class fare for the extra speed and the very special attention.

Karen glanced at her watch, a Cartier, before trying to concentrate on the menu. The aircraft was still on the ground at Kennedy, already ten minutes late for take-off. That fact increased her nervousness.

A half-page of aperitifs, half a dozen classic vintage wines, caviar and foie gras canapes, smoked salmon, a choice of tournedos of beef Bordelaise, cutlets, a cold plate . . .

She forced herself to take it seriously, making choices, even though she found it all ludicrous and nauseating, and – more important – even though she expected to eat none of it.

The aircraft was pulled by tractor into its taxying position just seventeen minutes after the scheduled take-off time.

The delay was due to the extra security checks because of a number of special passengers aboard, but this did not stop the captain cursing to his co-pilot and flight engineer in the cramped cockpit.

There was Jennifer North, star of a score of blockbuster movies, veteran of five marriages, and on her way to the London Clinic for a fourth highly-publicised operation; Andrew Muntwick Jr, son of the United States's reputedly richest man and flamboyant and attention-seeking where his father was reticent and anonymous; and General (four star) Ogden Peters, travelling incognito with his new wife on the way to a European honeymoon.

Two men had attracted suspicion at the check-in counter. The code letters ZTZ had been tapped on to the computer terminal to warn the guards at the departure gate, and the men had been taken away for close body searches. Nothing had been found, but more time had been lost.

Then a fourth special passenger had been led on board at the last minute – Anatoli Volkov, Soviet Deputy Foreign Minister, who had insisted on transferring to the Concorde when his Aeroflot plane, the only one at Kennedy at that time, had developed a fault.

Not least of the problems that raised was his armed bodyguard. That had been solved finally by a compromise of sorts in which he agreed to exchange his Makarov pistol for a specially adapted .38 for use in aircraft. The gun fired a special slug with a lethal range of only fifty feet.

Clearance was given for take-off. The aircraft began to accelerate down runway 31L, one of the two used by Concorde, and as the co-pilot called 'rotate', it left the ground and began to climb away at 200 knots.

The captain had quite forgotten the delay now as he

concentrated on banking the plane twenty-five degrees due south over the unpopulated wetlands of Jamaica Bay wildlife refuge to minimise take-off noise.

Karen sipped her Bloody Mary, and watched as the aircraft burst through clouds into brilliant sunshine. She had flown Concorde before and knew that for most of its flight, twenty thousand feet higher than conventional aircraft, they would be above the clouds.

The man across the aisle was still admiring her; she had placed magazines on the empty seat next to her to dissuade him from moving across to sit beside her. Was it her looks? She had always resented them; for a long time no one had taken her seriously within the movement, and even when they had, the first demands upon her were to make use of her body. Today, though, she had played on them. The clothes had been chosen carefully to frame her beauty: a simple white silk shirt, a grey skirt, an Yves St Laurent black and beige paisley shawl. All a long way from the jeans and men's shirts she normally favoured.

Taking care to avoid the man's eyes, she turned and looked back along the cigar-shaped compartment. She was seated near the back of the aircraft's first section. She could not see Vincent, but she could pick out his row of seats – about halfway down the rear compartment. She turned back towards the front. She could see the back of Simpson's head as he bent to retrieve a magazine he had dropped into the aisle. Nervousness? Was he as tense as she was?

She paused from her reverie to go through the charade of ordering lunch.

The hostess moved on, and suddenly Karen could not resist looking upwards. She hoped they'd got it right.

In the cockpit the captain and his co-pilot relaxed visibly, unclipped the top halves of their harness, tilted their seats and ordered tea.

The plane was now on autopilot.

The captain checked his watch. "With this tailwind," he said, "we won't be all that late."

Karen wanted a second drink, but did not order one. Although she had been told that the Beta blocking tablets she had taken to damp the tenseness would not react with alcohol, she dared not risk it at this stage.

Her eyes kept flickering towards her watch. No doubt Simpson and Vincent were doing the same. To occupy her mind, she pictured them the way she had seen them in the queue to board the aircraft: recognisable enough but, like her, looking different from normal. Simpson, very British looking, in his blue pinstripe suit and waistcoat, club tie, and scuffed briefcase, and eyes seemingly bored behind thick-rimmed spectacles. And Vincent, very changed, with a false tan and silk and mohair suit, slim black attaché case, and copies of show business magazines under his arm.

They would be watching for her to move, she knew. Forty-four minutes after take-off. One minute to go. The glass in her hand was empty, but she tightened her grip on it. For a moment she feared she would freeze.

Then she stood unhurriedly, as though about to visit the toilet, her right hand raised to steady herself. Her face impassive, she pulled at the oxygen mask compartment. It opened, but nothing happened. Despite the pills, she felt her heart quicken. She inserted her fingers, and the cold metal fell into her hand.

She sat and looked down, hiding the object from the aisle with her shawl. She doubted anyone had seen what she had done, but it would take them time to register and react and she would move in thirty seconds. Vincent must already be on his way to the tail of the plane.

The gun felt reassuring despite its tinyness; three and seven-eighth inches of semi-matte stainless steel, its barrel a little over an inch of that but fully rifled. It weighed four and a half ounces, no more than the glass she had held in her hand. The black ebonite grip was totally lost in her hand, but she knew this was no toy. The five .22 bullets that the mini Derringer held would be lethal enough.

A hostess was delivering more drinks. Karen waited for her to pass before sliding out into the aisle. It was easy to make out the Soviet minister's position, two rows of seats had been cleared for him and his bodyguard. His presence, which had not been expected, was a considerable bonus.

Simpson was already two yards ahead of her. He reached the front of the aircraft and wheeled, a revolver suddenly in his hand.

The Soviet minister's bodyguard moved fast, his hand leaping towards a shoulder holster. His fingers were not quite there when Karen leaned over the seat and shot him at point blank range through the left temple. Although the shot must have killed him immediately, she fired again.

She heard movement behind her and turned even though Simpson was covering the compartment. A man was on his feet. She heard the crack and saw the man thrown backwards across the seat. He lay, bent grotesquely, his feet still in the aisle, his hand on his chest. As she watched, his fingers turned red and his mouth began to make gurgling noises.

A passenger on the other side of the aisle moved as though to help him. "Leave him." Her voice was harsh.

At the rear of the aircraft she could see Vincent, standing in the aisle, his arm around a stewardess's neck, as he yanked her towards the intercom.

No one else moved and suddenly Karen felt wonderful in her power.

It was the first time that Simpson had been in a Concorde cockpit, even though he had studied the manuals, and he was glad to be reassured that the instruments – though larger in number than on other aircraft – were familiar enough.

He stood, gun in hand, over the three men. The captain and his co-pilot were seated side by side; the flight engineer was behind them; the fourth seat, on the rear port side, reserved for trainees and pilots in transit, was empty.

He quickly noted that the aircraft was on autopilot, and he

asserted his authority immediately. "Leave it," he had ordered as the captain's hand moved. "Touch nothing."

He knew that the pilots had orders to do what they were told in the event of a hijack, doing nothing to jeopardise their plane and passengers. But, theoretically, if the captain resumed manual control of the plane he could suddenly bank it steeply, throwing the hijacker off his feet. He would not risk it, of course. But better not to take any chances.

"Now take off your headsets," he instructed, "and switch to the speakers." Another precaution. He wanted to hear every message that came into the aircraft.

He noted the captain's eyes with wry amusement. He had established the fact that he knew his flying; the pilot must be wondering by now if he could take over himself if it proved necessary. A frightening thought.

He could not resist one more demonstration. He pointed to the buttons of the transponder, the gadget that provided the link with ground radar. By pushing the appropriate buttons the captain could produce messages on radar screens below. If he punched 77, for example, that number would appear beside the aircraft's radar blip on the screen, warning there was some unspecified danger.

"Go ahead," said Simpson. "Tap out 19. The current code number for 'we've been hijacked.' The captain's hand moved. "We should just be within Gandar radar range," said Simpson.

"What then?" asked the captain.

Simpson smiled openly. "Then we just wait," he said. "No one is in a hurry."

Out of sight in the centre galley, Karen unbuttoned her shirt, unclipped the front fastening of her brassière and removed the plasticine-like explosive.

Before returning to the aisle, she repadded herself with tissues – a small touch but she knew that the large breasts, like the wig that covered straight hair, the false mole on her cheek and the long fingernails, were all among the points that would be noted and feature in later descriptions. The more the police and the intelligence agencies could be deceived, the better.

In the main body of the aircraft, Vincent was the only man on guard, but the killing of the Soviet kept the passengers numb. And if there was any need for reminder of what could happen, there were occasional moans from a curtained-off section at the rear – the man who had been dragged away with blood oozing over his chest.

Conscious of the passengers' eyes, Karen began taping the plasticine-like substance on the walls and roof near the centre galley. She was surprised at how calm she felt now; she had risked two brandies which she had extracted from the drinks compartment, but it was not that. Psychologists who had studied terrorism – and she like all good terrorists had studied *them* in turn – had always claimed that women were more ruthless, more aggressive, stronger, less likely to give way to human feelings. That was why the command had given her this job: her first time in action, not counting the lone policeman she had killed in the Düsseldorf street to prove her commitment. As she fixed the lumps, using surgical tape taken from the medicine kit, she warmed herself in the knowledge that they had been right.

The detonating cord had been sewn into her waistband. She linked the lumps, and finally clipped the detonators into place – hidden, like the Derringer, by the mechanic they had bribed. It did not matter if they tracked him down; he had seen only one face, the money with which he had been paid had been well-laundered. His evidence, such as it was, would lead nowhere. If he were even alive by now, of course.

Her immediate task finished, Karen checked her watch again. She was suddenly nervous, tensed the way she was before an orgasm which would just not arrive.

For the first time she thought about how few of them there were and how, somewhere among the passengers, there might be one plainclothes guard undiscovered – or even some brave fool who might yet try to be heroic.

Her eyes roved over the passengers, daring them to meet her face. Most of them looked away – at neighbours, through the tiny windows out on to nothing, down at books or magazines they did not really see. Two had their eyes closed, and it amused her and gave her a new burst of confidence to realise they were praying.

Her eyes caught one man five rows away from her. He was watching her, his face still frozen in first shock. He was one of the ugliest men she had ever seen: pale-faced as though he had never seen sunlight, watery eyes, a straggly ginger moustache. Ridiculously, she tried to stare him down, but his eyes did not move. Angrily, Karen began patrolling the aisle.

It amused her how people moved their bodies inwards as she approached, afraid that the slightest contact might antagonise her. She reached the front, turned and fixed the Soviet minister in her gaze. Of all the passengers, he showed not the slightest fear; despite the events, he read steadily through a batch of papers as though nothing had happened. Either he was too old to worry about dying or – as Karen suspected – he rightly judged that he was too good a prize to be harmed.

His composure, though, added to the tenseness. She began to retrace her steps down the aisle, the small gun held at shoulder height, barrel pointing to the ceiling, like a duellist before turning and firing.

The ugly little man's eyes were still on her. From this angle, she could see that he was tubby, and she could make out a small sore underneath the hairs at the side of his mouth. He repelled and drew her; he reminded her of someone from long ago, but she had no idea who. Only that the subconscious memory was not a pleasant one.

His face was still fixed and expressionless. She could not know that it was only total incredulity even now: the man's mind had not come to terms with what had happened. It had drawn him inwards.

Beside her, someone moved suddenly and violently. Karen turned quickly, the gun coming downwards. There was a discernible click as she cocked it with her thumb. The movement had come from an elderly woman who, unthinking, had reached out to try to grab an empty glass that was falling from her table.

Karen felt herself quivering; the tenseness, the sudden fear, the anger were too much. They had to break. Quickly, she raked the end of the tiny gun across the woman's face. Its front sight left a three-inch line, at first a streak of white and then red as the skin parted.

Karen stood back, pistol readied. Her breathing was fast and audible. And then the ugly man moved. He began to rise to his feet. His face was still expressionless and his movements were almost those of a sleep-walker. He might not even have seen what had happened.

But Karen swung the gun back on to him. Hitting the old lady had helped, but the feeling was still there. She stared into the watery eyes. She wanted to kill, and she could think of no one she wanted to kill more than this awful looking man who stirred feelings from the past.

Vincent stopped her. He had seen what was happening, and had come forward. His free hand touched her arm briefly. He said nothing, but finally she lowered the gun a few inches.

Her eyes, though remained on the man's face. She wanted him to know how close he had come to death.

The captain was puzzled and increasingly nervous. It was over an hour since the hijacker had burst into the cockpit. Like all pilots, he had been schooled in detail on what to do: appear helpful but not friendly; try to keep the hijackers calm so they do not do anything irrational; co-operate with demands to relay propaganda messages, remembering that plans to defeat the hijackers were being made on the ground.

But these hijackers did not appear to want any help. The gently-smiling man who stood over them conveyed the impression that even the captain's presence was superfluous. Nor was there any need to keep him calm; he acted as though his veins contained iced water.

And as for propaganda messages, the hijackers so far seemed to want nothing.

There was a crackle over the loudspeakers: a request for information

The hijacker shook his head. "Tell them nothing," he said. "It's a try on."

He eased a packet of cigarettes out of his inside breast pocket with his free hand and lit one. His first. His hand seemed steady.

He smoked it right down, stubbed it out, and checked his watch.

"Okay," he said. "Radio ahead now and then prepare to divert to Shannon. Tell them we're landing there to refuel."

The captain reached for the microphone. "What if they refuse landing rights?"

The hijacker slipped another cigarette into his mouth.

"Then they've got it wrong," he said. "We're not asking anything. We're telling them."

# 2

Secretary of State Byron Fielding sipped his after-lunch coffee and reached for a cigarette before remembering he had stopped smoking.

It was his fifth day without a cigarette and at times like this – moments of the day when thirty-four years of smoking had conditioned automatic reflexes – he would swear it got worse each day.

He realised his wife was watching him and he smiled a weak smile. "I may not live any longer," he said. "But it's sure going to feel like it."

They were lunching alone at their Georgetown house, a rare event. He would study a number of situation papers and reports later, but apart from that the day was theirs.

Ruth pushed back her chair and stood. She was a strong, ambitious woman to whom her husband owed much of his success: without her drive he would probably have settled happily for a quiet academic life. Today, though, to fit the situation, she was being girlish.

She reached out her hand. "Come on," she said. "Let's go to bed."

"After lunch?" he grinned, accentuating the last word. But he took her hand and stood too, letting her lead him to the door. "You shameless woman," he said.

He paused at the foot of the stairs, released her hand. "You go on up," he said. "I'll get us a brandy. If I'm going to be seduced, we might as well do it in style."

He poured two glasses from the decanter in the study, paused and then began to sip one, delighting in the quiet and the unfamiliar luxury of idleness. He could hear Ruth upstairs. He would follow her in a few minutes.

He took another sip and rolled the brandy round his tongue. It was a particularly fine one, a gift from the French ambassador.

The grandfather clock in the hallway chimed two thirty, a comforting domestic sound. It seemed a perfect day, even without the luxury of a cigarette.

He finished his drink and poured a fresh one to carry upstairs. One of his predecessors, Dean Rusk, used to say, "While Washington is asleep, two-thirds of the world is awake, and I'm sure one-third is making trouble for us." Fielding was sure that applied to Sundays too – but today, thankfully . . .

He made for the stairs, holding the glasses carefully, suddenly beginning to feel murmurs of desire. He was halfway up when the telephone began ringing, the high-pitched warble that told him it was the direct line from the State Department. He paused, uncertain what to do, even toying for a brief second with the unthinkable possibility of disregarding it.

Finally, resignedly, he placed the glasses on the stair at his feet and made for the study. Until the moment he lifted the receiver he hoped that it was something he could handle with a swift, spot decision or could be delayed until later in the day.

Even many seconds into the telephone briefing from the chief duty officer at State's Crisis Center he managed to retain the hope. A hijacked British Concorde with Americans on board was troublesome, but the Department had a special section for such problems and there were also procedures for convening a special committee. As long as he was in telephone reach it would be enough to appear in person in some hours' time when the situation was more clear . . .

There was a pause at the other end of the line, and then the duty officer continued hesitantly, "There's something else, Mr Secretary sir . . ."

"Yes?"

"The Soviet Deputy Foreign Minister is on board . . ."

Fielding's hand went instinctively to his breast pocket for a cigarette pack.

He cursed.

"Mr Secretary, did you hear me, sir?"

Mr Secretary had heard. He would be there in fifteen minutes.

Forty minutes out of Shannon the hijacked Concorde began its descent. Simpson had taken the spare seat in the cockpit and sat silent the gun held casually on his lap. A few feet away the flight engineer had toyed with the idea of trying to overpower him, but not only were his orders specifically against taking such a risk, he realised that even if he were successful the others in the cabin could quickly demolish the aircraft.

There were bursts of conversation from the ground, but Simpson waved to signify that the crew should remain silent.

He waited until the aircraft was an estimated fifteen minutes from landing before he gave his instructions.

"Tell them you are landing to refuel," he said. "Anyone approaching the aircraft must be naked. And I mean absolutely naked. Not even shoes. Point out that we have already killed two people and will kill more if necessary. Tell them the aircraft is wired with explosives."

Then, almost as an afterthought, he added, "and tell them our call sign is changed. From now on we will answer only to the name Operation Nechayev."

In London it was nine forty-five p.m. when Concorde touched down at Shannon airport.

The British Prime Minister had swept into the Operations Room, 120 feet under the Ministry of Defence, less than ten minutes before.

At the time news of the hijacking had been received he had been on his way back to his residence at No. 10 Downing Street from a weekend at his country retreat, Chequers.

News would be relayed to Downing Street, but he wanted to be where the action was happening.

The Defence Minister was already there, standing, his arms folded, gazing up at a huge map of the Atlantic on which Concorde's flight had been followed.

A score of other people moved respectfully to an approximation of attention as the Prime Minister entered the electronically operated steel doors.

A loudspeaker stuttered into life. "All right Nechayev," said an Irish voice. "Descend at two hundred and fifty knots to five thousand feet."

"What's happening?" asked the Prime Minister, waiting until he was next to his Defence Minister.

The Minister gestured towards the speaker. "We're monitoring the aircraft," he said. "They're coming into Shannon."

"What's this Nechayev stuff?"

"God knows. You know what they're like, these terrorists, have to have their little touches. No doubt we'll know soon."

His voice was drawling, amused almost.

The Prime Minister turned, his face sharp, ready to criticise.

He stopped himself. The Defence Minister held the Right of the party. Foolish to clash with him unless he had to. He forced himself to keep his temper under control.

"Thank Christ it's not Heathrow," he said. "You've got everyone standing by?"

"The place is sealed off. It's like a NATO exercise. We'll keep it that way. They could still land there."

Concorde made a perfect landing at Shannon Airport at 21.37 local time.

Even though the Irish authorities had had little time to prepare, armed police and troops ringed the runway and marksmen were placed on the roof of the terminal building.

Armoured vehicles were still on their way, but five police cars were drawn up ready to block the runway if ordered to do so.

Special anti-hijack equipment – ranging from sensitive microphones that could be clamped to the outside of the aircraft to explosive spikes to deflate the aircraft's massive tyres – was already sorted. Three Special Branch detectives were dressed in mechanics' uniforms in case the hijackers relented on their demand that anyone approaching the plane must be naked.

Inside the cockpit, Simpson seemed as calm as ever and the captain wondered if he was drugged. He waited until the aircraft had taxied to a halt before giving his instructions:

"Listen carefully," he said, "because I do not intend to enter discussions. Tell them no one is to come closer than fifty yards except those handling the refuelling. And those men must be naked. I want that done immediately. There will be further instructions later."

He picked up the intercom, pressed the button and the woman hijacker answered immediately.

"Begin sorting them," he said. "And be careful. This is the time someone may panic." And then, as much for the crew as for the woman, he added: "Don't be afraid to kill again if necessary."

Despite the weather, cold and grey, the forty-first President of the United States was out on the practice golf course at Camp David when the call reached the communications cabin.

Fielding and White House staff had delayed calling him in the hope of more definite news, but now with Concorde on the ground at Shannon, it could only be time before the Soviets knew what had taken place. The President had to be told.

He listened for eight minutes without interrupting, asked four questions, and ordered "Keep me in constant touch."

Within two minutes communications staff were linking him, on the hot line, with, first, the President of the Soviet Union, and then the British Prime Minister.

As the refuelling began, Simpson gave the rest of his orders.

"I want the tanks a third full, no more," he instructed. "Tell them."

The Captain debated arguing; then relayed the message. The implication was clear enough and it should help those outside: the hijacker's destination was within about 1200 miles and would involve a landing on a short runway. It might be possible to make some preparations . . .

"The second is that the moment refuelling is complete I want landing steps. We will unload some passengers. But remind them that the slightest mistake and everyone is dead."

Again the captain relayed the instructions.

An Irish voice came from the loudspeaker. "Whoever is now in command of the aircraft, we would like to speak to you. What is it you wish?"

Simpson shook his head. "Tell them just to confirm they understand. There are to be no discussions."

He checked his watch. "Unless this aircraft is airborne in twenty minutes we will start shooting hostages. Five at first. Tell them that."

Ten minutes later passengers began surging down the steps on to the runway, pushing and stumbling in their haste. Their eyes blinked in the brightness as they neared the arc lights which had been set up in a circle fifty yards back from the plane. As they emerged, an army officer counted them aloud into a hand-help microphone that transmitted to the control room.

He reached fifty, and there were no more.

In the control tower the officer's voice was replaced by that of the captain, requesting urgent take-off clearance.

It was joined, on a separate speaker, by that of the army officer again. They've still got the Minister," he said.

"Clear them for take-off," ordered the officer in charge. He couldn't take any risks.

In the cockpit Simpson looked at his watch again. "Hold it," he said, with another of his faint smiles. "I'll give you two more minutes."

He gestured to the co-pilot and the flight engineer.

"You can go. The steps have been moved, but you can jump."

They looked at the captain, uncertain.

"Go!" For the first time Simpson's voice was raised, panic.

"Go on," said the Captain.

"We may need them," he said to Simpson, as they eased themselves out.

The smile was back. "Don't worry," said the hijacker. "You'll manage alone. And if not, I'll take over."

Normally at one o'clock on a Monday morning Soviet President Vasily Bukashev was back in Moscow after his weekend at his *dacha* beside the Volga.

A fur-carpeted, black Zil limousine would have swept him back to the apartment perched on Lenin Hills, overlooking downtown Moscow from across the river.

This particular Monday morning, though, he was deeply involved in a game of American poker with his friend and protégé Yury Voshchankin whom as President and General Secretary of the Communist Party he had recently made KGB chief.

The fact that Voshchankin was a friend was less important than that he was enjoying an almost miraculous winning streak, and for a man who hated to lose at anything that was enough to make him keep his minions wondering when he would leave, during the night or in the morning.

It did not for one moment strike him that the KGB chief could have been conspiring at his own losing hands, wanting to place the President in the best possible mood before lobbying a favour.

The call was a nuisance. He made to shrug the aide away, not knowing or caring what it was. In his hand he held three queens and two nines. There were one hundred roubles on the table.

Finally, the cards held tightly in his hand, he moved from the room to take the relayed message.

"Tell the President I will reply in ten minutes," he instructed. "I must think."

Back, seated opposite Voshchankin, cards placed on the table, he stared into space.

"What is it?" The younger man's voice was solicitous.

"Volkov, the fool, transferred to an English plane. No one dared stop him. It's been seized. Terrorists, it seems, but it is still airborne and there have been no demands."

"That was . . . ?"

"President Proctor. Volkov had been in New York." His voice was flat, concerned.

Voshchankin drew the wrong conclusion. "You've known him many years," he said. "I know you are close . . ."

Bukashev picked up the cards. Five minutes before he needed to call. "I raise you a hundred," he said. Then, "No, no, not just that," confiding. "Of course I worry for him, but think of everything he knows."

*If* Volkov could be persuaded to talk, there was no doubt of the importance of what he could say. His official position was not of the highest, but for fifty years he had been close to the centre of power, enjoying the confidences of many major figures.

Volkov's father, an early Bolshevik, had been captured by the British and shot attempting to escape from Baku in 1918. Others, attempting the same escape, had succeeded. One was Anastas Mikoyan, later President of the Soviet Union.

He had taken Volkov's son to Moscow where he had been brought up, the child of a hero.

The young Volkov had been dangled on Stalin's knee and, more importantly, early on learned the capacity to survive.

He had outlasted Stalin, Khrushchev, Brezhnev . . . Along the way the secrets he had learned had given him knowledge and influence beyond his position. "Our encyclopaedia," Brezhnev had called him.

Voshchankin shrugged. "He certainly knows where all the bodies are buried," and immediately regretted the phrase. He glanced at Bukashev but the President seemed not to have noticed. Then Bukashev raised his eyes. "Bodies buried," he said, showing that he had heard after all. "Very appropriate."

"The President asks what do I think. I would tell him if I could. I would do it if that aircraft were over our air space. I would like Anatoli Ivanovich back safe and unharmed. But I would not like him captive being asked questions by other people."

He threw his cards down and rose. "I would shoot that plane down. I would prefer him dead."

The aircraft's progress across the south of England towards Paris was monitored and relayed to the red-carpeted room in the Place Beauvau.

The Minister of the Interior, his chef de cabinet standing beside him, wriggled in a Louis Quinze chair and listened to the loudspeaker.

Responsibility for co-ordinating any action lay not with him but with the crisis suite on the first floor of the Quai d'Orsay.

But he had been dining nearby when he had been alerted about the hijacking, and there was always the possibility that the aircraft would land in France, thus involving him.

There was another reason. though, for his presence – the President would want to know whether there was anything special about the French passenger, André Labrosse, a very wealthy industrialist.

The Minister looked up. "All airports are alerted?"

"Yes Minister."

Another aide entered and began to whisper his report. He had been deputed to lead the enquiries about Labrosse. The Minister knew of him and his wealth, of course, mainly chemicals, centred in Lyons, not openly very political. But was there something else significant, something he did not know, but should? It was always best to be sure.

The report was a relief, although a few more checks were still in hand. Initial quick telephone calls to Intelligence, the Industry Ministry, the Party financiers, the local police had all yielded nothing worrying.

The loudspeaker came to life. "The aircraft has turned south, repeat south."

The Minister lifted one of the five telephones on his desk, the green one with the direct line. Time to reassure the President.

At fifty-one thousand feet, the lights of Nice almost immediately below, Simpson handed the Concorde captain the second set of navigational instructions.

Like the first they were written and contained very precise latitude and longitude bearings.

The captain began to flip the buttons that transferred the instructions into the computers of the inertial navigation system – the plane's directional brain, developed from the equipment that directed the Apollo astronauts so precisely to the moon.

Within ten seconds the computers had registered the information and changed the aircraft's course.

As before, there was no attempt at flying in regular airways, those channels of the sky like road lanes. All conflicting flights would have been ordered to keep well away.

"Algiers," volunteered Simpson. "Your flight's nearly over now, captain. Just keep up the good work. You've handled things very well."

The captain began to speak, but Simpson paused from lighting another cigarette to add, "No captain, keep concentrating. Still no small talk."

"I need to ask questions. You know that."

"I know your questions. Just listen. I'll answer them."

He paused. "As you surmise, it's not Algiers airport itself. It's a strip, ex-military, still I'm assured in reasonable order, well south, on the high plateau. The co-ordinates I gave you are precise."

The captain noted the word 'reasonable', but made no comment.

"How long is the strip?"

"About a thousand metres."

"You know I need more than twice that."

"I know the manual *says* you need nearly two thousand three hundred metres. We both know that allows for a massive safety margin. You can land it in a third of that, with luck."

"What about landing aids?"

"You mean beacons, radar? Nothing."

The captain's voice became incredulous. "What about lights?"

"Across the threshold of the runway, and marking the ends. They'll be enough." The voice was suddenly dismissive.

The captain concentrated on flying the aircraft. The descent had begun. Perhaps a half-hour now.

His mind ran through the problems. Normally an aircraft landed with precise directions and help from the ground on a runway that was well lit along both sides and at each end.

A threshold landing meant a row of lights *across* the strip at one end. The art was to aim for that row of lights. It could be done. The danger was going off the runway sideways, but the hijackers had anticipated that by providing lights marking the far end.

"I'll need one or two practice runs," he said at last.

"You'll have them."

All aircraft had been instructed to keep well out of Concorde's airspace.

Algeria, for long one of the terrorists' best friends, needed no prompting when it was advised that the Soviet Minister was on board: the USSR provided much of the country's vital technical and military assistance.

Nevertheless, two aircraft did follow Concorde's progress, but from eighteen thousand feet higher and forty miles in the rear – four times the limit for visual recognition even in daylight.

These two aircraft, though, Royal Air Force Tornado planes, were shadowing Concorde with the aid of what the pilots knew as visual augmentation – in essence a telescope that projected Concorde's image, greatly magnified, on to a small television screen. Its minimum-light system enabled it to operate in conditions of almost total darkness.

The pilot of the lead aircraft kept up a running report in code direct to the Operations Centre in London and from there relayed to the United States.

He reported Concorde beginning its descent, the passing over of the coast of Algeria, and – finally – the thin ribbon of light below, and the aircraft's positioning for an attempt at landing.

Jennifer North looked down at the sudden glimpse of light and giggled. She was stoned.

Ever since she had made the decision forty-eight hours before, Craig, her husband-manager, had been feeding her with regular doses of anti-depressant tablets. Since Kennedy she had been combining these with illicit and dangerous sips from the brandy flask in her bag.

Although she saw the lights, they hardly registered. Her thoughts were all inward. It had taken weeks to persuade her. The bad periods were interfering with her acting, they had said; were holding up shooting, were creating bad publicity from show business correspondents who hinted that her absences from the set were due to different reasons. Everything had been tried, they said. Well, almost everything. There was one more thing.

Craig had talked non-stop much of the evening and most of the night before she had finally agreed to the hysterectomy. The moment she had said "yes", lurched forward and sobbing, he had given her the first of the tablets. "They'll help," he had said. She must not be allowed to change her mind. The room and the surgeon were already arranged, had been for almost a week. She had held out longer than anyone thought.

She began to sob quietly and Craig, next to her, started to pat her arm. Her eyes were glazed, unseeing now. She doubted whether she would ever have had a baby; four marriages even by Hollywood standards was getting on to a lot of marriages.

But.

The hand on her arm tightened, hurting her, grabbing her attention.

There was another hand outstretched, palm uppermost, bright capsules in it.

"Come on," said the voice gently. "Take these."

The first two of Concorde's approaches were not really attempts at landing – they were the captain's manoeuvres to gauge the right rate of descent for a safe landing.

Each time he overshot, climbed, timed himself and made an 180 degree turn before coming in again.

He no longer worried about the hijack; the landing was everything.

"All right," he said after the second overshoot, "you'd better pray. I'm going in this time."

Through the cockpit window there was nothing to be seen as Concorde descended except the ribbon of light and the two lights further away.

The captain was coming in as slowly as possible, getting dangerously close to stall level, because of the short runway. Suddenly the lights were immediately ahead. The aircraft touched down hard and there were screams of tyres and machinery as the captain applied emergency braking and emergency reverse thrust all together.

The plane's own lights lit the runway. Yards before the lights that marked the end of the runway it came to a sudden, violent halt.

The captain's hands were sweating but his face was smiling. He had done it. Forgetting for a moment that it was all the hijacker's doing, he turned towards him, professional triumph on his face, waiting for praise.

Instead Simpson, already unbelted, was pouring liquid from a hip-flask into a paper cup.

He held it out to the captain with one hand, the gun raised in the other.

"Drink this," said the hijacker. "All of it. Or I'll blow your fucking head off. I don't care which."

# 3

The questioning of the freed passengers began immediately. The priority was trying to identify the hijackers in the hope this would give some indications of their likely actions and demands and their possible weaknesses.

Descriptions went on world circulation, with the greatest hopes being pinned on the two most specialised files on terrorists, those operated by Mossad, the Israeli intelligence service, and the Germans, and to a lesser extent on Interpol.

Two passengers had seen the woman remove the gun from the oxygen mask compartment and in New York and in London checks began on everyone who could have had access to the aircraft on the ground. The number with *official* access alone was frighteningly formidable.

Nevertheless, the investigations went on, even though many doubted they would prove necessary. At some stage the hijackers would have to show themselves . . .

Shortly after dawn the Algerian troops and armoured trucks took up positions in a circle around the hijacked aircraft.

Acting on strict orders from the Algerian President himself, who had already spoken to Washington, Moscow and London, they stayed well back. It was agreed by everyone that the first move must come from the hijackers.

The Algerians were accompanied by defence attachés from the British, French, Soviet and recently re-opened American Embassies. All four had mixed feelings: they resented being wakened so early, especially the Briton who had a hangover, but relished the drama in what was normally a dull, routine job.

The airstrip on which Concorde had landed was roughly one hundred miles south of Algiers itself in an arid, gloomy-feeling part of the country with nothing but dry earth and stones, dirty yellow flat-topped hills, and the occasional muddy rivulet produced by the winter rains.

By late morning the attachés and the troops had done all they could. Radio links had been set up; soldiers crawling forward in camouflage uniforms had clamped microphones on to the outside of the aircraft; and a negotiating team – including an English psychologist who specialised in siege situations – was on the way.

The demand when it was finally made came not from the grounded aircraft but in three identical notes, one delivered to the Soviet mission in Geneva, another to the American Embassy in Paris, and the third to the British mission to NATO.

"They're showing us how organised they are," said Byron Fielding.

"They've already made that abundantly clear," said the President's National Security Adviser, Leonard Meyer.

It was six twenty-two a.m. Washington time; Fielding had slept the night at State. Meyer had just joined him.

They sat in the small conference room off the main operations area of State's Crisis Center. On the wall before them was the screen, displaying now the typed message.

"You have forty-eight hours beginning noon GMT today to satisfy the following demands," the message began. It was typed in block capitals.

"At least we know what they want," said Fielding. He was clutching a cigarette. Giving up smoking would have to wait until this crisis was over.

Meyer shrugged. "I can't see it makes any difference." He turned to the others around the table. "I don't see how anyone can give way."

The normal Crisis Center staff had been joined by a

specially-convened team of terrorist experts, and by representatives from the Soviet, French and British Embassies.

Meyer stared up at the screen at the rest of the hijackers' demands. Part was for money. But that hardly mattered. What they wanted most was the freedom of seven terrorist leaders captured in Spain two and a half months previously.

Meyer reached for a sheet of paper and ran through the names.

"Flynn, Michael O'Dare. Born Galway 1954. Arrested Royal Ulster Constabulary 1977, charged killing three British soldiers, jailed for life. Escaped 1978. Arrested Chicago 1980, held on warrant complicity murder of Earl Mountbatten. Released lack of evidence. Suspected involvement in airborne destruction of Aer Lingus 747 1982 in which 211 died – claimed reprisal for Eire-UK agreement over extradition of terrorists. 1983 – believed on loan as training officer to Corsican separatists. 1984, suspected complicity in international terrorist raid Geneva airport, fifty-seven dead . . ."

"Hassan, Abdul. Real name unknown. Born 1959? Lebanon? Numerous terrorist acts culminating in assassination of head of the PLO 1983 on behalf of breakaway group after PLO-Israel talks. 1984, shot in counter-assassination attempt. Not seen again until arrest. 'Official' Palestinian organisations said to have a one million dollar 'contract' out on him . . ."

"Titov, Viktor. Born Ukraine, Soviet Army, defected East Germany. Joined Red Army Faction, West Germany, 1978? According to informants key technical figure in same-day murders of KGB and CIA chiefs of station Paris 1982. Major proponent of spreading 'war' eastwards. Planning, but not operational, involvement in scheme to dump nuclear waste in Odessa Harbour . . ."

Meyer shook his head. "The only names missing are Jack the Ripper and the ghost of Adolf Hitler . . ."

"They should have been got out of Spain," said Fielding. "Dispersed. It's madness keeping them together."

For two and a half months a dozen nations had been

arguing their cases for being handed individual terrorists. While the discussions went on the seven were in the maximum security wing of a high security prison that the Spanish had built only a half-dozen years before to hold Basque terrorists.

"It would have made no difference," said Fielding.

He picked up a pastrami sandwich, left from the previous night and now curling in the heat, and bit into it.

He looked up at the bank of clocks that showed the time in six different capitals.

One showed London time, thirty minutes after noon. An hour earlier in Algeria. He tried to picture the scene, and lit another cigarette.

"Why did the crazy bastards do it?" he said, half to himself. "They must know we can't give way. Any of us."

Although it was still a month to the start of the hot season when temperatures would top forty degrees centigrade, by noon the sun was already roasting. Those watchers who could found shade beside trucks and Land-Rovers from which to stare out at the desolate scene.

The aircraft, a huge, gleaming white bird, its tail tipped with red and blue, stood incongruously against a landscape of rock, soil and alfa grass which stretched as far as the eye could see.

This was the Algeria of the nomads, seemingly boundless, a land of bluffs and cracked hollows, of biting cold in winter and of scorching heat and sandstorms and locusts in summer.

The soldiers smoked and talked softly between themselves, as though subdued by the strangeness of the scene. At first it had been almost amusing, an exciting change from the routine, a chance for action. But now uncertainty had communicated itself; it was obvious that those in charge had no instructions other than to wait.

Inside Concorde it was hot too, and the smell of a score of bodies confined in a small space was beginning to grow.

It was also quiet; the occasional sound of the shuffle of a

hijacker's feet, the scrape of matches as one chain-smoked.

No one went near the centre galley where explosive was taped to the walls. No one had checked it for well over a dozen hours. In the heat the tape worked loose, and the mixture it held in place began to sag. But no one came.

The leaders of the three countries most involved – the United States, the Soviet Union and Britain – all reached the same decision individually and collectively very quickly.

American policy, formulated in the mid 1960s, had always been not to meet any demands, no matter what was at stake. The rationale was simple: that this was the only way in the long run to discourage terrorism. A price had been paid: in the half-dozen years to 1974 alone ten diplomats were murdered when the US government refused to pay ransoms. Other diplomats, though, supported the stand. Without it, they were convinced the number kidnapped would grow to hundreds.

Other countries gradually adopted the same line: Israel held firm when ninety children were held – with the result that twenty died; the Germans accepted the death of Hans Martin Schleyer rather than give way. More recently the Vatican had refused to pay ransom for the Papal Legate in Brazil.

And the Russians had always taken a totally non-negotiable line with terrorists: Soviet airline pilots, for example, unlike their Western counterparts, were ordered to let the aircraft be destroyed rather than give way to hijackers . . .

President Proctor came to the decision after talks with Meyer, Fielding and his Defence Secretary. Also present was Bill Watson, his Chief of Staff, an anonymous, non-publicity seeking figure in his Administration, but the man he consulted most.

"Okay," Proctor said, summing up, "we try to keep the hijackers happy while we get a force in there. Then, with luck, we bust everybody out."

He waited for nods of approval.

Bill Watson was the only person who spoke. "I know we all go along with that, Mr President, but can I suggest just one small change. It *is* a British aircraft even though most of the passengers left aboard are American. Now . . ."

The President listened. And finally smiled.

The Soviet President had wandered down to the Kremlin's situation room, four storeys below ground. He had come to a similar conclusion.

Non-committal at the start of his conversation with the American President, he had allowed himself to be 'persuaded'.

Bukashev gestured to one of his aides to open one of the bottles of Narzan mineral water that stood on the green felt conference table.

He waited until he had the glass in his hand and then asked the officer in command, "What's the latest news?" It was a foolish question because anything important would have been relayed to him, but he wanted to be seen to be taking such interest in case Volkov did die. The man still had many friends.

"Very little, Comrade President. The only messages from the aircraft are warnings to stay clear. The speaker, for the first time, is one of the hijackers. Both we and the Americans are attempting to match his voice with voice-prints. The microphones placed by the Algerians point to two, possibly three other hijackers on board. The passengers are strangely quiet – we fear they must be bound and gagged."

Bukashev turned to Voshchankin and led him to a corner. "Are there any leads from the questioning?" The KGB had already seized nearly 400 dissidents believed to have connections or sympathies with terrorism for interrogation. Voshchankin shrugged. "It takes time, but nothing yet."

"And Nechayev? Does that lead to anything?"

Both knew who the man was, or rather had been – the nineteenth-century philosopher on terrorism and author of the handbook the *Catechism of the Revolutionist*, a frightening list of principles for revolutionaries to adopt including one

Voshchankin knew by heart: "He is an implacable enemy of this world, and if he continues to live in it that is only to destroy it more effectively."

Now he spread his hands as a gesture of not knowing. "Maybe trying to be ironic because Comrade Volkov was on board. More likely, trying to impress their knowledge of revolutionary history. For all their danger, they're often intellectually very childish."

Bukashev looked at his watch – a gold Rolex, a gift from the Americans to mark the signing of some pact.

He had to make contact with the President again, to convey his reaction to his suggestion.

He took Voshchankin's arm and led him towards the private elevator that led to his office.

There were still forty-nine hours until the hijackers's deadline.

In the elevator he confided the Americans' suggestion to the KGB chief: that the British should be persuaded to send in a Special Air Services team to try to free the hostages.

Voshchankin waited until they were in the President's wood-panelled office.

"Why the British?" he asked.

"Because it's their aircraft and because they are experienced in this kind of thing. Only the Germans and the Israelis have the same kind of skills – and we could hardly ask them."

He leaned forward and rang for coffee.

"And we will, of course, insist that they are accompanied by three of our men. I believe the Americans will make the same insistence. President Proctor and I obviously share the same thoughts."

The coffee came, almost immediately.

"It seems an ideal solution. If the rescue succeeds, our men come home as heroes with Anatoli Ivanovich. We can always convince our people of the crucial leading role they played . . ."

"But if it fails. If Comrade Volkov dies . . ."

"Then," said President Bukashev quietly as he lifted his

coffee cup, "we blame the stupid British for their ineptitude."

It was exactly the advice Bill Watson had provided for his President.

# 4

As if to reinforce the American involvement in the rescue attempt the SAS team took off from the United States Air Force base at Chicksands in Bedfordshire, an hour from London, in a C-5A Galaxy troop and cargo plane.

Major Jonathan Hyams, forty-two, a veteran of the Yemen and of Ulster, and his twenty men were almost lost in the vast aircraft – but it had been chosen so that it could be used as a theatre for briefing when it landed at a NATO base in southern Italy.

Each of the men on board had received special training in storming hijacked aircraft. They practised regularly on mock-ups of all the major types.

Before leaving England they had one final exercise, using one of British Airways' other Concordes and a wooden replica of the interior. In it, they had triumphed – in nine and a half minutes from start to finish.

That, though, thought Major Hyams, as he settled down on the aircraft, had been without the complication of the Americans and the Russians he had been ordered to take along.

These men – three from each country – would join them in Italy. They might or might not be good at their jobs, but Hyams knew that was secondary. What really mattered in an operation like this was that every man knew exactly his role. It was a precision affair like high wire acrobatics at a circus. One man slightly out could wreck everything.

The Russians and the Americans were waiting when the aircraft landed in Italy. The groups entered the aircraft and took up positions well apart from each other.

The Americans' ranking officer, a colonel, endeared himself immediately. He had, in fact, been chosen partly for his public relations skills. *If* the attack succeeded, and *if* the colonel survived, he would be perfect on American television . . .

"I just want you to know that we'll do exactly what we're told," he said to Hyams. "We've no illusions why we're along." He nodded towards the three Russians. "You may find them harder, but I'd guess they know what it's about too."

The briefing began almost immediately. Large blackboards, a movie screen and cases of equipment were set up in the aircraft.

It lasted almost an hour, during which the men were shown diagrams and maps of the area, detailed photographs, and cut-outs of the plane showing where, it was believed, the passengers were located.

"We thought at first that they were bound and gagged," said the officer conducting the briefing. "But from analysis of the sounds on tape we're now virtually certain that they're being kept under sedation. That should make your task easier, and harder. They won't be leaping all over the plane when you get in there. At the same time it's not gonna be any good you shouting for them to hit the floor."

The mock-up model of Concorde's interior was six feet long. Passengers were represented by white dolls.

"How sure are you of their location?"

"Pretty sure. We're picking up their breathing. You'll get an update when you get there."

He prodded four black dolls with his baton. "The hijackers," he said. "One more than we originally thought. They move about, of course, but this is where they seem to settle at night." Three were in the front compartment with the passengers, the fourth in the cockpit with the captain. He was the one in contact, desultory though it was, with the Algerians outside the aircraft.

The rest of the briefing followed smoothly: a resumé of the time situation, an assessment of the hijackers' possible mental states by a psychiatrist, detailed information about the Algerian troops who surrounded the aircraft and the orders they had been given . . .

Finally, it was over. The major was glad. It had been necessary, but now he just wanted to get on with it.

"Any questions?"

A long silence. Then one of the Russians looked as though he was about to speak, but changed his mind.

A shuffling of feet, a gathering of equipment, some muttered expressions of 'good luck', and twenty minutes later the Galaxy was on course for Algiers.

It landed at a military base seventy-four miles south of the airstrip.

They travelled the rest of the way by truck.

The time chosen for the rescue attempt was five thirty a.m. – six and a half hours before the deadline expired, and the time, it was judged, that the hijackers would be least on their guard.

At a whispered order, two SAS men crawled towards the aircraft. The plane, surprisingly, had never been immobilised, and their task was to drain off Concorde's hydraulic fluid.

The major waited for their return and then checked the latest electronic intelligence reports on the positions of the passengers and the hijackers.

Finally satisfied, he peered around in the darkness, raised his hand to his second in command and began crawling forward.

It was five twenty-seven a.m., three minutes to zero hour.

Twenty feet from the aircraft most of the SAS men froze, while a small group continued forward. These men held explosives and small scaling ladders.

The hand on the major's watch reached five twenty-nine.

The explosions ripped open two of the doors. The SAS men were inside the doorways within fractions of a second, tossing in stun grenades, grenades that would produce no fragments but whose sound and flash would immobilise anyone inside for perhaps six vital seconds.

"Down! Down!" Though the shouted order might be pointless, the SAS men yelled it out of habit.

From 120 yards away from Concorde a monitoring unit studied the scene through infra-red glasses.

The commentary they gave was relayed direct to London, Washington and Moscow.

The President, his Chief of Staff, the Secretary of State, the Defence Secretary and the National Security Adviser all listened to it in the Situation Room under the White House.

"They're in. There's firing. Now it's quiet. It seems to be over."

There was a long silence and Fielding stared up at the second hand of the huge clock that faced him.

Projected on a screen, adding to the filmic quality of the situation, was a huge photograph of Concorde on the air-strip.

"We're receiving news from the rescue mission now," the voice went on. "Reports say one hijacker dead. Looks as though he committed suicide the moment the attack commenced. All passengers seem to be safe. Doctors going in now."

In three capitals there were smiles of relief. Three leaders would all claim credit.

"Well, gentlemen," said the United States President. "I think a drink would be in order . . ."

"I think some medals would be justified," said the British Prime Minister.

"Make sure Volkov is on the way back as quickly as possible," instructed the Soviet leader . . .

The monitor's voice filled the loudspeakers again. It was puzzled. "Will you repeat that? Please will you repeat that?" He was obviously talking to the raiding party on board the plane.

There was a pause. Then, "Will you repeat that? Please check and repeat."

In three capitals, men waited and wondered, knowing that something was wrong, but not knowing what.

At last they heard.

"Rescue party reports one person dead, one woman slightly injured, rest well," said the monitor's voice. "But only twenty-one passengers and crew aboard and one hijacker."

The voice rose. "Three hijackers and five passengers unaccounted for." Despite his training incredulity coloured his voice. "They've vanished!"

# 5

The search for the missing eight people began immediately. Air and sea ports were sealed; spotter planes searched the vastness of the Sahara to the south; trucks crossing border points were searched.

But there was little real hope of finding them this way. It was obvious that the hijackers and their prisoners must have left the aircraft between touchdown and the arrival of troops a little over two hours later.

This meant that they had a start of almost forty-eight hours – plenty of time to reach a port or another airstrip and be well away from Algeria. On the morning Concorde landed there had been no checks. Why, the authorities consoled themselves, should there have been? It was taken for granted the hijackers were all aboard the aircraft. The hijackers could have driven away without problems.

There were many possible escape routes, and all were being checked. The most obvious was for the hijackers to join the N40 road, the main east-west road through central Algeria and head eastwards. There was not a single town for almost a hundred kilometres. They could then have turned north, just one truck (for that was the obvious vehicle) among many using that road.

The five missing passengers comprised the three obvious ones: Volkov, Jennifer North, and Andrew Muntwick Junior. The fourth was André Labrosse, the wealthy French industrialist – taken, it was suspected, because of his nationality: another government to pressure.

The fifth was a mystery for several hours until reports of

the questioning of the freed Shannon passengers were received. The man was named on the passenger list as Alfred William Ross, American, of Westlake Village, California.

He seemed a complete no one. Why should the hijackers have taken him? Then came the reports of the clash between Ross and the female hijacker. It began to make sense. Five was the number that the hijackers had decided to take – the number they could handle. The woman had probably insisted on taking Ross in the absence of any other obvious figure. And, after all, it might be a clever move: Ross could represent Mr Average, the man in the street.

The names of the five were released on Saturday, 30 March. One woman, Janet Peters, watching lunchtime TV as she cooked, realised the identity of Ross.

But it was the weekend, and she did not know that no one else in the Agency was aware that Ross hated his first names and always called himself 'Edwin' and that the California address was his sister's – he always used it on forms because he had moved home so often.

Intelligence, the FBI and the police were all, of course, interested in filling in the background on the missing Ross. In Westlake they had drawn a blank. His sister and brother-in-law were away; none of the neighbours knew much about Ross beyond the fact that he lived east and was something in computers.

The FBI circulated Ross's brother-in-law's car number, and then everyone turned to more important things. Not knowing that Ross was the most important thing of all.

President Proctor had thought hard over whether he should stay in Washington for the weekend or go to Camp David. If he went to his retreat it would show that the leader of the world's greatest nation was not going to have his routine disturbed by a handful of terrorists. On the other hand, if he stayed it would show that he cared. He decided to stay.

Muntwick was in many respects his biggest problem: his father was by far the Party's greatest benefactor, and his influence was far ranging and deep. Whatever the hijackers demanded – whether it was a repetition of their earlier one or a new one – there was no question of giving way, of course. But facing Muntwick would be difficult. Thankfully, he was away visiting some of his interests in Asia. There were attempts being made to contact him now.

Proctor sat behind his desk, stiffly erect on the vast green leather swivel chair, and squared a pile of blank writing tablets. Apart from them, a pen set and a telephone the desk was bare.

He picked up the pen and scribbled himself a reminder. Only then did he look up and acknowledge the presence of his Chief of Staff, and the heads of the FBI and CIA.

"All right," he said. "Brief me."

The CIA chief leaned forward to hand over a folder, but the President let it lie on the desk, "No," he said. "Tell me."

One after another the CIA and FBI chiefs detailed what was happening at home and abroad.

Passengers were still being questioned, and photofit pictures were being put together. The aircraft was being fingerprinted. Checks were continuing on people who might have had access to the plane. In Algeria, police were searching through files on foreigners who had entered the country within the previous month . . .

The 'explosive' taped on the walls and ceiling was fake – children's plasticine, the reason it had not been picked up by the explosive-sniffing machines.

The major possible lead so far was the dead hijacker. "It's pretty certain he shot himself. He had to be some fanatic to let himself be left alone. There was only one way out for him. We're trying to identify him now."

"What about the passengers? Do we know how they were sedated for so long?"

Cord Warren, the CIA chief, answered. "Valium," he said. "Pure, ordinary valium. Nothing clever. They were made to drink valium syrup soon after landing. Then the one hijacker on board kept them topped up with intramuscular injections. The doctors reckon pretty heavy doses, maybe thirty milligrams a time – that'd keep anyone out. That's why it was a good drug to use. You get a lot of latitude; hard to overdose anyone."

"Why didn't anyone know there was only one hijacker on board?" asked Bill Watson. "I thought those bugs they put on the outside of the plane could pick up anything."

"Tape recorders inside," said Warren. "We found three. The hijacker we found dead kept them running, occasionally moving them, we'd guess, frequently changing tapes – they found a dozen near his body. The sounds included sighs, whispers, the noise of a body moving in a seat, the clatter of a glass . . ."

"Don't the tape recorders provide any leads?"

Warren shook his head. "All identical – the pocket jobs combining calculator, watch and timer, much favoured by travelling businessmen. But mass produced, cheap. The kind of stuff that's flooded the market since the micro-chip really got underway. Maybe Hong Kong. All identification burned off with acid."

"Okay, but why'd they go to such lengths? Why so complicated?" asked the President.

Warren inclined his head towards a fourth man seated beside him who had so far remained silent. "I think Dr Rosen is best qualified to have a stab at answering that."

Rosen was a psychologist who specialised in terrorism, advising governments and corporations on dealing with hijackers and kidnappers.

"We can only guess, Mr President," he said. "But I would say it's probably a good guess. With any hijacking the longer it lasts the harder it gets for the hijackers. The art, as you know, is to wear them down. Let them beat themselves. Over the years it has been remarkably effective. For that reason, some terrorist groups have preferred kidnapping. That way they are not pinned down, they are not so to speak in the hands of those who surround them. But kidnapping has a slight disadvantage. It's not generally so spectacular." He spread his hands. "Look at this current case. Where else could you kidnap such a group?"

"And so?"

"What I'm suggesting, Mr President, is that these terrorists, whoever they are, have combined the impact of a hijacking with, for them, the advantages of a kidnapping. I would say they've been very clever."

"All right." The President pushed back his chair and stood. "Keep me in touch." He nodded to his Chief of Staff. "Tell Bill here if it's anything important. He'll see I get it immediately."

The others rose to leave. Proctor's voice stopped them at the doorway. "One thing I forgot," he said. "Why'd they take the body of one of the men they shot?"

The corpse of Volkov's bodyguard had been found at the rear of the plane, covered with a blanket. Despite the fact that another passenger had been seen to be hit in the chest, there was no sign of his body.

"We're still looking," said Warren. "We think maybe he was still alive and they wanted to get him away from the plane before shooting him. Then they'd have dumped him. That's the best we can guess at right now."

The injections always worked quickly on Andrew Muntwick Jr, but for some physiological reason there was a brief period between them when he was awake and alert.

Not once was there a chance to do anything, but even if there had been he would have made no attempt at escape.

Never in his life had he been left unprotected. He was not afraid of being harmed now because he could simply not comprehend it.

Apart from discomfort, what feelings he had were almost of amusement. His non-arrival in London – where he was due to watch the recording of a pop group in which he had bought an interest – would inspire excited talk and publicity (it was his father, not him, who tried to keep his name out of the newspapers).

It pleased him too that his bodyguard would now be punished for not keeping Muntwick Jr within his sights, allowing him to slip away to the airport. The man had always been too zealous. The boy had bided his time.

And there was pleasure in imagining his father's feelings. Muntwick Jr had never been in any doubt why he had been conceived, produced like something from a test tube.

Now let the old man pay.

The news did not reach Muntwick's father until Sunday, 31 March, a full week after the hijacking.

The reason was that he had taken elaborate steps to cover his own movements, even from his own headquarters in Chicago.

At a time like this it did not pay to trust anyone. For Andrew Muntwick, far from being on an Asian tour, had been holding secret discussions in China, finalising talks that had gone on spasmodically for years, giving Muntwick's corporations the first-ever licences to begin helping China exploit its natural resources.

The message was received only after he was airborne out of Peking on his way back to the United States aboard his personal 747.

His face remained expressionless as he read the message. "Tell the captain to head straight for Washington," he ordered. "And radio ahead. Give our arrival time. Make sure the President sees me as soon as I arrive."

The aide took the instructions without surprise. He was used to such imperious commands.

The aide was one of ten people on board, a group that included two stewards, a doctor and two nurses.

The aircraft had been divided into a series of communicating rooms that comprised a lounge, a small bedroom, an office, staff quarters, and a small medical clinic that was wired for instant satellite communication with New York Hospital-Cornell Medical Center to which Muntwick had, pointedly, given large sums of money.

Muntwick himself sat in the lounge, slumped in an easy chair, his feet spread out in front of him. Despite several days of hard negotiating he had a clipboard of papers on his lap – problems he had had to set aside until now.

He was seventy-three, six feet eight inches tall, thin and only just beginning to stoop. His face was almost albino white – not through illness, but because he feared the sun: he was convinced it caused not only skin cancer but a range of other diseases.

Beside him was a bottle of iced Perrier water, all he ever drank, whether by itself or to accompany his meals of vegetables and wholemeal bread. Until he was in his late fifties Muntwick had been a hard-living, heavy-smoking, heavy-drinking man. Then he had been forced to have a laryngectomy, an operation for the removal of the larynx and vocal chords.

The need for this owed nothing to his living pattern, and in fourteen years since no other serious illness had befallen him. But it made him feel mortal.

The device he had had to wear since the operation served as a constant reminder. It was a small case mounted on his upper chest, and consisting of a valve system that regulated the air flow from an opening in his neck to another in the windpipe. With its help he was able to produce rasping but understandable speech.

Muntwick closed his eyes and put down his glass. He could have been sleeping, but his mind was still trying to come to terms with the enormity of the tragedy. Andrew Jr should never have moved anywhere without his bodyguards. Muntwick did not even know the boy was planning to go to Europe. He had waited until his father was away.

Muntwick had married late in life, aged fifty-one, and not for love but after a search conducted by a string of advisers. His new wife had not known what was involved. Muntwick's plan was that the marriage should last less than a year, the time it needed to produce a child. He did not mind whether it was male or female as long as it was his seed. Due to the difficulties that the two had in producing, the marriage had lasted through three years and a dozen specialists. The divorce proceedings began three weeks after the boy was born. The mother's settlement, which included a 200-acre estate near Palm Springs, contained a written clause that she should never give interviews nor reveal anything about the few years she spent with Muntwick. He had not seen her since.

He opened his eyes, and pressed one of the buttons on the arm of his chair. Lunch arrived immediately: the steward had been waiting outside the door. It was a dish of raw vegetables, and a glass of tomato juice. Muntwick picked up a piece of celery.

He tried to read as he ate, but found it hard to concentrate.

He began thinking of Proctor – a good man, a middling President. A man he had spotted early and, to say the least, helped. It takes money to get on in politics; millions to make President. In the early days Proctor had found it hard to attract money. Potential backers had doubted his staying power; there were rivals more desirable. But Muntwick had seen that Proctor – and his family – were never short of funds, even though it had involved complex and devious methods of injecting them to hide the true situation. Later, when it looked as though Proctor was a winner, others had come along. But there was no disguising the fact that Proctor was beholden to him – and that Muntwick knew more than enough to be able to destroy the man's re-election chances if he ever 'leaked' all he could.

Muntwick's hand tightened on his glass. It was obvious what the President's reply to the hijackers had to be: total refusal of their demands. But Muntwick didn't care about countries or ideals or a President's pride. All that mattered was that when he was dead his son should go on.

He had no doubt Proctor would see him as soon as he returned. He had found Proctor, fed him, succoured him, led him by the hand into office. And, by God, if need be, he would destroy him just as readily.

Two discoveries were made before noon Washington time on the Monday.

The first was about the shot passenger whose body had mysteriously vanished.

It had not. He was the same man as the hijacker who had

killed himself. The autopsy revealed the reason why he had been so ready to die and also, later, his identity. He had terminal cancer, certainly no more than a few months to live. Further checks revealed that he was an American, living on Long Island – Douglas Nash, thirty-four, married, two small children, and a clerk in a loan company.

Investigators reconstructed the scenario: Nash had been used because he was dying. At the same time the other hijackers had used him in a second, earlier role – to pretend he had been shot. The reason for this had to be that with the exception of the woman's .22 Derringer the weapons the hijackers had carried were not real, just imitations, made of wood or plastic, that would not show up on metal detectors. The 'shooting' of Nash had been to prove the reality of the weapons. "All it needed," said one investigator, "was a loud yell, a capsule of theatrical blood, and a bit of squirming about."

The second was the finding of a twenty-seven foot four-berth power cruiser, waterlogged but still afloat, in the Mediterranean, a few miles east of Barcelona. The hijackers' attempts to sink her had failed. The boat, later found to have been stolen in Corsica a month before, was deserted. It would have been a routine boat theft, one of scores, except for a clip of matches, embossed with the Concorde emblem. One of the prisoners had stuffed it down the side of a chair – all he could do.

Leads were developing, but no one knew how much time they had.

At about the time that Andrew Muntwick was sitting in a suite at The Mayflower, fuming and waiting for Proctor to be available, Officer Glenn Webb of the FBI was deciding that he was running out of leads in the area assigned to him.

Even though it was not his direct responsibility, he was aware that little was being done about Alfred William Ross. On his own initiative, and because he had a *feeling*, he began to probe.

The first step was re-reading the passengers' statements, a

few who had occupied key seats had agreed to undergo hospitalisation where their brains were probed with an electrode, a technique neurosurgeons had found stimulated memories.

Webb stopped at one statement and read it again carefully. It did not register at first. One of the other passengers, seated across the aisle from Ross, had seen him reach in his pocket for a handkerchief and with it bring out some change and keys by accident. They had fallen on to the floor and the other passenger had helped him retrieve them.

Webb re-read the passage three times before he realised its significance – according to the other passenger one bunch of keys had been car keys.

If Ross had left his car at home would he have carried the keys to Europe? No, Webb decided. He must have driven the car to the airport.

He traced it within the hour. And from the registration number he obtained another address, not Westlake Village this time but Ross's home.

There was no one there. But a search provided the name of a company where Ross was said to work – the Vibart Systems Agency Inc. in Washington DC.

It was listed: Webb called the number. At the other end of the telephone a man listened and then said, "Please stay where you are and I'll call you back."

Ten minutes later Webb did receive a call, but not from the man with whom he had spoken but from one of his own chiefs.

Two hours after that a grey-suited man with the expressionless look that Webb knew so well was asking just why the FBI man was interested in a man called Alfred William Ross.

The President had an iced bottle of Perrier water waiting standing in a silver bucket when Muntwick was ushered into a side gate, through the rose garden and into the White House.

The industrialist feigned not to see it, refused a seat, and launched straight into his half-prepared speech; the right, he thought, of someone who over the years had handed over in excess of $150 million to the party – apart from up to $1 million a year to Proctor's personal campaigning.

"I'm a sad and worried man," he began. "I've come here to tell you I want my son back."

Proctor reached out and touched the older man's arm. "Andrew," he said. "We're doing all we can, but –"

Muntwick cut him short. "The solution is a simple one: ask them what they want, then give it to them. Catch them later. Just like any hick cop would do in any kidnapping."

"We don't even know what they want yet."

Muntwick's voice was impatient. "They'll want money. What was the first demand? Fifty million? Give it. If the United States can't afford it I'll pay it." Fourteen years before *Fortune* had estimated Muntwick's personal fortune to be between $1400 million to $2500 million. Today it was considerably more.

"And they'll want prisoners – terrorists, Andrew," interjected the President. "Men who have killed and will keep on killing if we let them be released."

"Nonsense. A few more madmen on the loose won't make any difference."

Proctor fought to keep his anger under control. Presidents were not spoken to in this way. But not only did he not want to jeopardise the flow of Muntwick money, he genuinely feared the old man.

"They're not even in this country, Andrew," he said, trying to reason with him. "They're in Spain."

"The Spanish will do what they're told, and you know it."

"But the Russians. They would never agree to giving way."

"Screw the Russians. They're pragmatists. Do a deal with them. There's always something they want: technology, cheap loans, grain, some spies returned . . ."

"Andrew, I can't. We can't back down. The greatest nation on earth cannot capitulate to a few thugs, particularly now. You must see that."

Muntwick's cold eyes held him.

"No excuses," he said. "No excuses. I want my son back." Muntwick lifted his hand and pointed dramatically at Proctor. "Get him!"

He turned and strode to the door. The President's face was purple with rage, and he felt bile in his stomach. No one could treat him like that. His mouth opened but no words would emerge.

He was still speechless when Muntwick slammed the door on him.

Webb's visitor, who had introduced himself as Dixon, managed to keep his voice calm despite the mounting realisation of what had happened.

"You have a description?" he asked at last.

Webb consulted notes. "Height, five foot four–five foot five, weight around one hundred and fifty pounds, brown hair, faint moustache, pale complexion . . ."

"You have finger prints?"

"We've got prints taken from where he sat. His will be among them. There's maybe a dozen others as well, though. You want them?"

"Please. As soon as you can."

"We're checking all the prints on the computer anyway . . ."

Dixon lit a cigarette, placed it carefully in a short black holder and tapped non-existent ash into a tray. "You won't find them on the computer – not yours anyway."

"He's one of . . . ?"

"If I could have them."

An hour later there was no doubt.

Dixon requested and was granted an immediate appointment with the head of the security section of the National Security Agency. He in turn saw the director of the NSA who insisted on seeing the President's National Security Adviser.

And he saw the President.

"News?" asked Proctor.

"Not direct."

The President turned away. Then Leonard Meyer's eyes told him there was more.

"Well?" he asked.

"This man Ross who the hijackers have. You know, Mr Ordinary."

The President had absorbed the briefings well. "Yes. Personal animosity. Broke the elementary rule in dealing with hijackers not to antagonise them . . ." He began sorting through papers to find a note.

"He's more than that, Mr President."

"What is he?" After the tension of his meeting with Muntwick the President began to laugh skittishly. "The Pope in disguise, the Party Treasurer absconding with the funds . . . ?"

Meyer's voice held no amusement. He managed to keep it even but it was still imbued with the tension he felt.

"Mr President," he said, "he knows about Operation Whiphand."

# 6

Ross lay on his back and stared upwards at the naked bulb that hung well above him.

His face itched with the stubble of unshaved beard but he struggled to keep his hands away, he had already torn the skin, scratching in his sleep.

It was two days since he had last been injected with drugs, but standing was still an effort and from time to time he drifted off into a half-sleep and hallucinations of waves breaking on a beach.

The room in which he was confined was tall, about twice a man's height, but narrow and only just long enough to hold its one piece of furniture, the bed.

It had, he thought, been especially partitioned off to become a prison: one wall was crudely made from planking. Much of the time he could hear the sound of voices from the next room but he could make out only the occasional word. He had seen nothing of his fellow prisoners.

He eased himself up on the iron bedstead, moving his eyes from the weak bulb that had already become a symbol of his captivity. As a prisoner, he had begun smoking again after seven years. His captors had left cigarettes as a matter of course; food had been harder to get. After a few hours he had taken one.

They were American cigarettes and the packets had no tax stamps. A Duty Free shop? An aircraft? He extracted one from the pack, lit it and filed the piece of information in his mind.

It might help the police when he was freed – if he was

freed, of course. But more importantly, mentally filing pieces of information would help occupy his mind, give him the feeling that he was doing something positive.

The smoke made him gasp and he realised that it would soon make the small room unbearable. In a sudden gesture he stubbed out the cigarette and tossed the rest of the pack towards the end of the bed. Damned stupid to start again.

His recollections were hazy. He could remember the flight, of course, and the hijacking and – most vividly of all – the moment when the woman had turned the gun on him. For several seconds he had thought that she would shoot him. In a strange way the fact that she was so beautiful had made it even more terrifying.

He remembered too the landing at Shannon, the new fear when he was one of the two dozen passengers not unloaded there, and later being forced at gunpoint to drink the sweet syrup.

After that, though, memories were dreamlike, fragmentary. There had been a boat, he was certain of that. And he thought he remembered a forest and the smell of wet grass; and, later, darkness and the throb of an engine – the back of a sealed truck? He knew there were other prisoners – he could recall their shapes. One was a big man, he thought the Soviet minister. But did he know that? Or did he surmise it because it was obvious?

The travelling seemed to have taken days: there had been changes of vehicles; sometime he had been half carried, sometimes dragged. He had never been fully conscious.

Each time he had hovered on the brink of consciousness there had been the needle. At first he tried to fight it. Later it was almost welcomed – it gave rest and stilled the fears.

There was noise outside and a small hatch in the wall was opened and a mug and a piece of bread thrust through. The hatch was closed again immediately. Ross leaned over, took the mug and drank thirstily. It was hot and burned his mouth, and the coffee was weak, little more than hot water, but he welcomed it. He paused and dipped his bread into it and then, despite his hunger, made each bite of bread last as long as he could.

Two days since he had arrived here – he was reasonably sure of that, but not certain. Without light and with his body rhythms affected by the drugs, he had arrived at his estimate by counting meals. His kidnappers might, of course, be serving them at odd intervals and times to confuse him, but he doubted that. In the few contacts, in the little things he had noted, they seemed to show a strange rigidity.

He finished the bread and the coffee and wished there were more. He leaned over to bang on the wall, but his hand stayed still. He thought he could withstand the isolation, he had always been a solitary man. But he was afraid of the woman. He did not know whether she was outside or not. He would not risk provoking her.

Ross feared her in the way he had been afraid of monsters and witches as a child. She was an unknown evil. There was more. He had never before seen such hate for him in anyone's eyes, that moment she had levelled her pistol on him.

He suspected she would kill him without much thought. He had little doubt her presence was the reason he had been taken. Surely he could not be regarded as much of a catch compared with all the other people who had been on board the plane.

Or did they – and the thought struck him for the first time – did they know something? Impossible. Even he himself only suspected. But if they did . . .

He lifted the empty mug to his mouth before remembering he had finished every drop.

And if he thought they would kill him because he was of no negotiating value, would he tell them . . . exchange his secret for his life?

The Americans, the Russians and the French all received separate messages on Friday, 5 April.

They were all posted locally to the Embassies of the three countries in Brussels.

The demand was identical: $100 million in cash; the freeing of nineteen listed terrorists, including the ones held in Spain; and the placing of full-page advertisements (text to be supplied later) in a specified list of newspapers.

With each demand there were Polaroid photographs – Volkov for the Russians, Muntwick, Jennifer North and Ross for the Americans, Labrosse for the French. The photographs appeared to have been taken in a cellar, and the subjects all looked drugged.

A deadline was given: midnight, Friday, 19 April – two weeks away. The messages, all typed and on the same machine, said there would be no further communications unless at noon GMT two days before the deadline expired a message – again specified – was broadcast on the BBC World Service News.

If that were done, further instructions would be delivered. If not, the hostages would be 'executed'.

President Proctor was still discussing it with Bill Watson when the second communication reached him.

"They're giving us some time to try to find them," said the President with a confidence he did not feel.

"Time to sweat and start a lot of in-fighting," said Watson.

The intercom sounded. "Mr Cord Warren, Mr President."

Watson looked quizzically at his chief. "He said he'd something important on what's happening. I told him come on over."

"Send him right in," said Proctor.

Warren's message was brief. An agent code-named 'Pike' had filed a report of a meeting with one of his Soviet KGB contacts. The information itself was not presently verifiable, but the contact had a high reliability rating for past information.

In essence, his claim was that his Soviet masters were letting it be known discreetly that they were prepared to enter into private negotiations for the return of their minister, while pretending to be continuing with the three-power ones.

"He's that important?" asked Watson. His expertise was political realities at home and keeping the President on the right track. Outside the broad guidelines he cared little about foreign affairs.

"They must be afraid someone'll get him to talk, the way they have with some political captives in the past. Knowing the way their minds work, they might even be running scared that we'll try to do a private deal to get our hands on him with no one knowing."

"But so what? He's only a deputy minister . . ."

"It's not his job that matters. It's everyone he's known, all the secrets he's got tied up. There aren't many survivors at the top around the Kremlin. He's one – has been for forty years. He must be a walking encyclopaedia. There must be a lot of people in Moscow mighty scared."

"We'd like him?"

Warren shrugged. "We'd love him. But even if he came on offer I suspect my advice to you Mr President would have to be that the risk was too great."

"Still, as you say, the Ruskies don't know that."

"No, and there are always others. The Chinese, the Albanians. And there'd be a wide market for any information . . ."

"But no intimation that they're after Ross too?" asked the President, joining the exchange.

"No, sir, but . . ."

"But *what*?"

"We've no reason at all, not one in a million, to think either the terrorists or the Soviets know what they've got. But no one can be one hundred per cent certain. But that's not the major fear."

"Which is?"

"Ross himself. We're getting personality profiles put together, getting psychiatrists to advise how they think he'll cope under stress. Initial feedback is comforting. It's reassuring in itself that he's a computer programmer and by all accounts a good one. The job calls for just those qualities that might help him now: the ability to cope with dull routine most of the time but to be able to come up with something ingenious when it's needed."

He paused for reactions. There were none. He continued in the same even tone. 'I won't pretend there isn't one big fear, though – what'll happen if the moment comes when he's convinced they're going to kill him. Precisely because they think he's Mr Nobody they might kill him first, just as a warning, keeping their valuable hostages in reserve.

"He's not a fool. He'd know what was happening. In any event, his captors would probably taunt him. That's been the pattern in the past."

"So?"

"So, Mr President, we've got Ross thinking he's about to die because he's the most expendable hostage. Yet he knows that he's got something, that he's not as valueless as they think. He's not even sure quite what he's got, but he knows it's something. My feeling is that at such a time he might try to make a bargain . . ."

The President leaned forward and instinctively touched the secret report that Watson had put together that morning on the frantic lobbying that Muntwick was conducting with Party officials. He shivered.

"Cord," he said, "We *must* get them back."

"But you said yourself, Mr President, that we daren't give way."

"That's right, Cord. I daren't." The voice hardened slightly. "So find me a way. You've got the best brains in the world for this kind of business, as you keep telling me. So prove it. Just prove it."

# 7

The options were all on the President's desk within twenty-four hours. There was one copy only and that was delivered by hand by Cord Warren himself.

The President read it through without comment and passed it to Bill Watson. Watson read it and in turn passed it to Leonard Meyer, the Security Adviser, the fourth occupant of the room.

They were seated not in one of the White House's more formal rooms but in a simple garden room, a room that Proctor had had equipped with a desk and a few chairs and where he spent a lot of time, claiming that the rudimentary surroundings helped remind him what was really important when making decisions.

The memorandum that he had been given covered two and a half pages. There were only three options listed and after each of them a summary of the advantages and disadvantages.

Proctor did not need to stare at the notes to recall them. They were simple enough.

The first called for him to make a personal approach to the Soviet leader Bukashev. He would then assure the Russian that while the United States remained totally opposed to yielding, it recognised the special problems this time of the USSR. *If* the Russians wished to persuade the Spanish authorities to release the prisoners and if it wished to pay the ransom, the United States Government would understand . . .

Proctor discounted that one immediately. The option

sheet listed only one other major advantage – that it would be seen as a Soviet backdown. But there were several disadvantages, not least the possibility that the Soviets would be suspicious of such an offer and produce some reaction that could not be foreseen. The greatest, though, thought Proctor, was that such an exercise would help the Russians get their hands on all the captives, including Ross, if it were successful. And if they did know anything . . .

The second option lay in trying to blackmail the blackmailers, specifically by trying to seize in turn terrorists who could be exchanged for the prisoners. This, though, was dependent on first finding out who the hijackers were in order to determine what other terrorists they would worry about. And then there was the practical problem of actually finding and seizing the necessary terrorists . . .

Not, thought Proctor, a very viable option.

The third, though, was interesting.

He leaned over the desk, picked up the memorandum, and read it again, conscious that he was being watched.

"Give the hijackers what they want, but not in such a way that we appear to do this.

"Any such scheme would involve, first, persuading the hijackers to reduce their demands to the ones considered major.

"To specify, their demands for the purposes of this memorandum can be divided into three:

"One. Money. This should present no problem in that the sums demanded could be provided privately. Andrew Muntwick had already made it clear that he is willing to pay. Additionally, both Miss North's studios and the Labrosse companies carry kidnap insurance. In the circumstances, the hijackers could even be offered *more* than they ask in return for reducing other demands.

"Two. Media advertisements. This is a minor problem, even though some compromise would be necessary. For example, announcements could be carried in newspapers within the United States without loss of face of the Administration provided it was made known that this was the only concession the President was prepared to make. No doubt other friendly nations could be persuaded to adopt a similar stance. A further possibility is specially one-off copies of *Pravda* and *Izvestia* which could, of course, be handled here with existing facilities."

Proctor's eyes lingered long over the third and final point, and he had no doubt that the other three were watching, studying his reaction.

"Three. The freeing of prisoners as listed in the demand. The number totals twenty-nine: six in Israel, five in France, four in Germany, two in the United States, five in Russia . . .

"Plus, of course, those held since January in Spain. These, the subject of the original demand after the hijacking, are the key figures. It is suggested that offering the freedom of these people alone together with the satisfactions under One and Two above would constitute a large enough bargain to free the hijacked.

"If the prisoners in Spain are to be freed as part of such a deal there would appear to be two possibilities other than, of course, simply giving way.

"The first would be to persuade the Spanish Government to release the men (not a difficult problem for either the United States or the Soviet Union), and announcing that they were taking the step of their own volition to help their friends.

"The second possibility involves clandestine activity, and would appear to carry more dangers. However, such dangers could be reduced to a minimal level by operating through third and fourth parties.

"This possibility would involve the freeing of the prisoners held in Spain without the United States seemingly being involved itself.

"In other words the United States should – indirectly – arrange for the prisoners to be broken out of prison. There are precedents for such an action. (See Appendix Two on the freeing of Ambassador Jackson after being held by the Tupamaros.)"

Finally Proctor looked up, the memo still in his hands. He removed his spectacles and rubbed his eyes.

"Well, gentlemen?" he said.

"Option three looks the only contender," said Watson, "but I can't pretend I like it."

Proctor stared at Meyer.

"It could work, provided we can get a message to the terrorists and they agree."

"And, of course," said Watson, "if we can break those guys out – but in a way so removed from us that no one would know even if they were caught."

Proctor, Watson and Meyer all turned to face Warren. He was seated in a small rocking-chair, and finding it hard to look dignified.

"I think it can be done," he said. "As a nation we've got a lot of resources – even if we have to disguise them – that the terrorists haven't got. That is if we want to spring these guys from jail."

"But what about keeping the United States, the President, out of it?" asked Watson quietly. It was his main concern.

Warren had thought about it carefully.

"We'd make it look as though Andrew Muntwick was behind it, had set it up personally," he said. "That wouldn't be difficult. I'd suggest that we actually get him involved."

"But who'd run it, who'd head things?" asked Meyer.

"I worried about that," said Warren, "but I think I know the man."

"What is he?" said Watson. "Some kind of suicide pilot?"

It was meant as a joke, but he was surprised at the serious look on Warren's face, and the flat tone of his voice.

"Something like that," he said.

# 8

A man does not voluntarily quit the CIA at the age of forty-five when he is regarded as one of the leading up-and-comers and when only two years before he has been awarded the National Security Medal by the President in a very private ceremony.

Not unless, of course, someone else like a big corporation has heard of you and makes you an enormous offer.

That was what George Singleton's colleagues in the Directorate of Operations – the clandestine side of the company – thought at first, although he volunteered no information.

When, months later, casual callers at his rambling house in Cleveland Park noted that he did not appear to be doing anything, there were rumours that he had been ordered to retire. His crime? The rumour provided a number of contending ones until they died down: that he'd failed his regular polygraph test, that he was suspected of passing information to Israeli intelligence (for like many operatives he felt the US was leaning too far towards the Arab nations), that his son had done something that would make Singleton blackmailable if it became known to the Soviets . . .

The truth, though, was more prosaic, and though he had spelled it out to his superiors in resigning he had never made it general knowledge, even when he knew of the rumours.

A side result of this attitude was that those superiors who knew his reasons retained a special respect for him.

Singleton simply did not like the way Intelligence had gone, was going, and how it was treated by successive Administrations and their appointees.

Singleton had joined the CIA from Harvard Law School in the sixties and had received his grounding in the Cold War: the Berlin Wall, the Cuban missile crisis, two events which as a newcomer he had watched from the sidelines, but both of which had influenced him; the early days of American involvement in Vietnam when his early convictions contrasted strongly with his later disillusionment.

He had found the work as exciting and as satisfying as he had hoped, operating under cover in the Dominican Republic as rebellion flared; moving to South Africa after Verwoerd was assassinated to direct investigations over whether Verwoerd's death might have been part of a Soviet-backed conspiracy, a task judged too sensitive for men on the spot.

He had done well. He had served in the key places, gradually emerged from behind the scenes. His work alone would have taken him high, but other things helped: his father, now dead, had been in Intelligence, in the OSS, before him. Singleton had married another CIA employee, his boss's secretary, early on.

And because of a mixture of luck, dedication and lack of political ambition, he had come unscathed through various attacks on CIA staff: the going of James Jesus Angleton, Singleton's 'perfect' Intelligence operative, forced to resign after disclosures of the CIA's domestic spying; the breaking up, in the late 1970s, of 'the old boy strain' in the agency by Admiral Turner, President Carter's CIA chief . . .

Gradually Singleton's disillusionment grew. It was the simplest of things: the feeling that, for the wrong political reasons, a job that had to be done could not be done properly. And as a man of black and white emotions he felt he had to be in or out.

Imbued with what his Russian opponents would have called *toska* – world weariness – he took surprise advantage of an early retirement scheme and quit. Because he had said nothing, most of his colleagues were surprised. They would have been marginally less stunned if they had seen the inside of his private study. Over the months before quitting, he had suddenly begun clipping cartoons about the CIA. There was no shortage. His favourite, which he had had photographed and enlarged, and then framed dated back to 1979, one of the years of low morale. It showed a man in a hat and a trench coat, 'CIA' on his arm, writing over and over on a blackboard, 'I am not supposed to murder anyone anymore.'

It helped that he could leave without problems. The pension was not inconsiderable, though not on its own enough. But he was only forty-four. Not that there was any real need to work – the house, left to him by his father, one of those rare beings, a native Washingtonian, had never carried a mortgage; after sixteen years his wife had left him for a West Coast realtor and was not seeking alimony. There was still his son at college to support, but he had always saved and invested wisely in stocks.

It might, he sometimes thought, have been different had Debbie lived. That might have held the marriage together. His son, perhaps, would have blamed him less; perhaps he would have blamed himself less. He knew he had to be away that week she was ill. It was his job. It would have been no different had he been an insurance salesman or a newspaperman. Nevertheless, he wasn't there and because of his job the news had taken a long time to reach him. The Priest the company had sent along had told him everyone felt guilty about something when a loved one died, and he supposed it was true. But it didn't help much.

Now he was alone, and it was a measure of how far he had gone that mostly he did not mind. Since his retirement he had drawn more into himself. Even his immediate neighbours saw little of him. They had grown to accept his existence without his company. When they thought of him it was in terms of a 'mild eccentric'. Their main curiosity on the odd occasions when he was discussed was where he went when he left the house in the morning long before most people were awake. The answer to that was prosaic. He drove down Wisconsin, out along the Potomac, and watched birds.

On Sunday, 7 April Singleton rose soon after four, packed a sandwich, a flask of coffee, a half-pint of brandy and his binoculars, and well before five was pulling his car to a halt.

It was a favourite spot, especially around dawn, where he could breathe in the cool air, delight in the silence of the marshes.

A redheaded woodpecker rose in front of him. Normally he would have raised his glasses to admire its beauty, but this morning he waited silent in the half light, drawn back into cover, the binoculars and his bag at his feet.

He held a Browning high power pistol lightly in his right hand. He hated carrying it – two and a half pounds of extra weight and bulk – but he had done so since retiring. It was, he accepted, his duty. Many of the things he knew were still highly classified. If anyone ever tried to seize him, they had to fail. Either he fought them off or he died in the attempt. Except on the range, where he kept in practice, he had not once fired the gun, but he knew it worked well. He checked it every morning, a daily habit that had become as mundane as cleaning his teeth. He had chosen the gun because of its close-range reliability and for the number of rounds it took: thirteen.

The road was too far from where he stood for him to hear traffic. But he judged that the car he had noted following him should be parked by now.

Gradually his eyes acclimatised. He had positioned himself well. Whoever came towards him would have to negotiate a narrow track that passed less than twenty feet away.

Of course, whoever it was might not follow. They might simply have pinpointed his destination. It might be a 'dry run'. They might wait at the road. The target might be his car.

He could only wait and see. But that he had been followed was not in doubt. The car, a dark blue Chevrolet, had picked him up in Georgetown. Its driver had showed signs of skill, but it was a hard time of day to tail someone, particularly a man like Singleton who for twenty years had checked instinctively for such things as other drivers look out for traffic cops.

Singleton's breathing was soft, and despite his readiness his muscles were relaxed. He was pleased with himself.

A black-bellied plover took off, surprising him with its sound. It became still again, and he was beginning to doubt anyone would come when the man appeared.

He was dressed in a grey tweed overcoat, a shapeless country hat almost obscuring his face. He walked carefully but clumsily – a man unused to being away from paved surfaces. His head moved nervously from side to side.

Singleton had already settled into a stance: feet spread about shoulder width apart, toes pointed out for balance. Now, in one movement, he locked his knees tightly, raised the pistol and levelled it in a two-handed grip.

Still he said nothing. There appeared to be only one man, but there was no way of being sure of that. Let the man come closer.

Then Singleton realised that despite the difficulty in walking it caused him the man was holding his arms out, stretched as though to demonstrate to anyone watching that he carried no weapon.

He paused and for the first time Singleton recognised the face.

"If you're there, George, as I guess you are, I'd be obliged if you didn't shoot me. The President's got enough problems without having to find a replacement for me."

A crooked smile broke on Singleton's unshaven face. But he purposely waited for what must have seemed a very long few minutes to the motionless man.

Singleton liked Cord Warren, but he wanted to make the head of the CIA sweat a bit.

They sat facing each other on the bank, the coffee, sandwiches and brandy on the ground between them. There was only one plastic cup and Singleton had filled it to the top with a mixture of coffee and liquor.

Warren took the first drink from it and almost gagged on the alcoholic strength of it. Singleton bit into a sandwich and seemed not to notice.

Warren had not seen his companion for nearly two years, and that the only time since Singleton had quit. The CIA man had not been Director then; his appointment had been made a few months later. Singleton had sent him a brief note of congratulations – sincerely meant. He might have his doubts about Warren himself – too ready to go along with the fiction of détente, like the Administration – but it was genuinely good to see a professional back at the top.

"You look well," said Warren at last.

Singleton raised his hand and stroked his chin. He had not shaved for three days. "The Hemingway look?" He smiled.

"You're still alone?"

"Yes, the divorce went through, but I guess you knew that. I feel pretty good. I thought it would break me up, we'd been married a long time, you know. But God help me, Cord, I found I liked being alone. I even felt guilty at first."

"And Betty?"

"She seems to like it pretty good too. Whether it's the climate out west – she never liked being back in Washington, you know – or having someone around who can talk about his job I don't know."

His eyes watched Warren's face closely to see if there was any hint that the CIA chief knew about Kate. Nothing. But he was sure he could not. He had gone to great lengths to keep it a secret, and he was an expert.

Singleton turned his attention back to the scene around them. Quickly he raised his glasses. "A parule warbler," he said moments later after watching its flight.

"You come here a lot." A statement.

"As you know, or you wouldn't be here. Two, three times some weeks, always around this time. Funny thing is that I feel I need less sleep all the time – four, five hours a night is fine."

"And you think?"

"Not much. I just look and enjoy and marvel. Sometimes you get the feeling it must have been like this soon after it all began." He kept his binoculars trained at the sky. "Wonderful creatures, birds. Compared with them we're just newcomers, Cord. Ones not very much different from the ones we're looking at now were flying about at least seventy million years before we were even around. Just think what they've survived: changes in climate, in the earth's surface. And think where they've gone: over the Poles, into the deserts, across the oceans, high into the mountains."

He put down his binoculars and picked up another sandwich, but he didn't eat; just continued talking.

"And they run the whole range from generalists to real specialists. You'll find house sparrows anywhere there are humans. Or you can have real specialists like humming birds – long bills and tubular tongues so that they can suck nectar from the heart of flowers but not eat solid food."

Warren was surprised not only at the passion in his companion's voice but also how unembarrassed the other was in saying such things. In their agency days together he had found him tight lipped. "A man with water, not blood," someone had once called him.

"You're getting pretty philosophical in your middle years," Warren commented at last.

"Philosophical enough to sit and wait patiently, engaging in small talk until you get ready to tell me what the Director of the CIA is doing soon after dawn sitting on the ground trying to look as though he wouldn't rather be home in bed."

Warren stretched out his legs and took another gulp of coffee. He felt its warmth relax him.

"George," he said, "I came here because I have a story I'd like to tell you."

"George," began Warren, "I want you to imagine that you're back a couple of years – not long after you decided on Out."

"Remember that SALT II's been around two to three years and it's already pretty obvious that the Ruskies got more out of it than us, and that we'd had other problems with them – not least Afghanistan. Okay? Nevertheless, the President insists on going ahead with SALT III. My predecessor, the Chiefs of Staff, a lot of good thinkers, put forward their reservations, but politically it's a good move for him."

Singleton nodded but said nothing.

"That's by way of background just to remind you where we are. Now we switch our attention to South Carolina State University, an okay but kinda second league place. We don't know it at the time but what's going to make it special to us is that the Professor of Pure Mathematics, a man called Thomas Charlton, has a passion. Charlton at this time is easing up to retirement, is very much Division Two, like the college.

"Thing is that he's got a passion: the factorisation of large numbers, a mathematician's intellectual game, if you like. To you and me it may sound a weird kind of thing to be excited about, but I'm told that mathematicians have been fascinated by it for hundreds of years. In fact, the best method of factorising large numbers until Charlton came along was produced by an amateur with just such a passion."

Singleton nodded and lifted a hand to interrupt. "You're going to tell me what factorising is, I imagine . . ."

"Sorry, George. I've had so many briefings, I forget. Sure, sorry. Factorising a number is working out what sets of numbers multiplied together could make up that number.

"Now to someone like you or me that sounds pretty easy until you think about it. But I'm told that given a big enough number – and that's what we're talking about – there are literally billions and billions of possibilities. A computer could do it – given a few million years!

"What mathematicians like Charlton have looked for over the years is a mathematical formula that provides a shortcut, something that will help you get it right pretty quickly some of the time.

"The prize for doing this? Some praise – and envy – among your colleagues, some footnotes in the text books . . ."

He paused while Singleton poured him more coffee and brandy.

"Okay. That's part of it. Now I have to ask you to switch to something else.

"Back in the mid-seventies – and you may remember the

papers we circulated around the company at the time – some men at Stanford came out with a new idea for ciphering messages.

"They called it the public key or trapdoor system, and the important thing as far as this story is concerned is that a bit later people at MIT went on further and made a practical system based on the great difficulty of factorising really large numbers. They claimed – after a whole load of research – that to break such ciphers would take millions or even billions of years even using the most powerful computers, the kind that NSA have over at Disneyland.

"What they didn't know and what we didn't know until later was that the Soviets had been investigating the same possibilities and coming to the same conclusions.

"What must have got them excited was the thought of something that for all practical purposes was one hundred per cent secure, but also fast and easy to use.

"Now about five years ago we start to get intimations that the Soviets are using a trapdoor system for the vast majority of their top secret coded messages: diplomatic, military, Intelligence, you name it.

"You know that although we've been able to crack the ciphers of pretty well all the minor powers, except for odd cases this hasn't been true of the Russians. They're just too damn sophisticated.

"And their move over to using this trapdoor system doesn't help us. We can't break that either. So the NSA boys go on doing what they've always done, taping everything they can, storing in case one day . . ."

He paused again. "I'm sorry it's so complicated," he said. "But I thought you'd better have it all."

"It's okay, I'm following."

"All right. Now I have to ask you to switch back to Professor Thomas Charlton and his passion. Thomas Charlton at two twenty-five a.m. one morning is still in his study playing around with numbers and eureka, he suddenly thinks he's succeeded. He's found a new way of factorising large numbers. Not every time, but some of the time.

"Now think on that, George. Here are the Ruskies using a cipher that's based on the secrecy of two numbers that multiplied together make up the third. That final number isn't secret, that's why one of the names is the one I mentioned, the public key system.

"And here's Professor Thomas Charlton with what we'll call the Charlton Algorithm. Now he's excited, but of course he knows nothing of its Intelligence significance, and of course he needs to test it.

"To do this he needs to get to work on the computer. He knows how to programme one but it's been a long time and he's a bit rusty and impatient. He seeks out an old friend who is a programmer for a small software company. He prefers not to use anyone on the campus because he's made a mistake before.

"The tests come up trumps. What Charlton finds is that using his new formula and making the computer try three hundred million different combinations he can get the right answer around three to four per cent of the time for the size of numbers one uses for cryptography. Now, that sounds a hell of a lot of combinations to a layman like me, but they tell me at NSA that our modern computers can handle that in a few minutes.

"Charlton's pretty excited by now of course, but he's still cautious and before taking the next routine academic step of circulating it around some other mathematicians for comments before publishing, he mails one copy only to an old friend at MIT who has the same passion.

"In his letter Charlton couldn't resist a joke. 'Remember,' he wrote, 'all those papers from Stanford and MIT back in the seventies and early eighties about a new unbreakable cipher. It's a good thing we didn't put them into use.'

"Charlton's friend – and his name isn't important – went to Washington the same day. He had, and has I guess, an NSA contract, and although he knew nothing about what the Russians were doing he recognised the significance of what had been done.

"The result, George" – Warren's voice had become

quieter and more dramatic – "is that for almost two years we've been breaking Soviet ciphers. Not all of them, of course; about three or four out of every hundred.

"But think of how many even that is – think of the thousands of radio telegrams pouring in and out of the KGB Centre alone every day of the year. Then there are the diplomatic messages, the army, the navy, the air force . . .

"And it's the best grade of information, George. What did someone once call it? The words of your opponents speaking in secret to themselves.

"They may have the balance of military power, but this gives us the edge over them. We *know* what they're up to a hell of a lot of the time, and the beauty is they haven't the faintest idea."

"It must have been kept a tight secret."

"You bet. The President, of course, a handpicked few in the Administration, a few in Intelligence, a larger number in NSA, but even here the minimum . . . I can tell you the total. Until we started to speak eighty-seven people, now with you eighty-eight."

"All American?"

"No one else is even getting a hint of this, no matter how close an ally. NSA are even purposely not playing over old tapes – though they'd love to – in case taking them out of storage raises any suspicions."

"And what happened to the professor?"

"He was picked up, persuaded not to publish, given a prestigious job. The military won't believe that three to four per cent is the limit. They think with work he'll come up with something even better. He's happy to devote himself to trying. He gets everything he wants."

"So what's the problem? Why make me secret holder eighty-eight?"

"The programmer Charlton used when he wanted to test his algorithm on the computer."

"Why wasn't he given a job too?"

"He was: one of the NSA front firms they use to help keep tabs on the outside world. They tried to persuade him it was just because of his talent, but no one could be that big a fool. Not only did it coincide with helping Charlton, but then the professor moves and his paper is never published. And, of course, he'd have been quizzed discreetly as part of his general questioning whether he'd put anything on paper or discussed it with anyone . . ."

"So?" Singleton prodded gently. Despite his heavy clothing he was getting cold.

"So he's settled down, and told the standard things, like don't have an anaesthetic except under one of our doctors, and don't chat to strange men at conferences, and don't ever try to take a holiday behind the Curtain . . . Hell, you know the drill."

"So?" Again gently.

"So nobody worries when he takes off on a simple holiday to Europe." He raised his head and stared into Singleton's eyes.

"Not, that is, until he gets himself hijacked."

# 9

Back home Singleton fixed himself a scotch and water, removed a steak from the freezer and opened the lounge windows out on to the garden.

It was twelve thirty on what had turned out to be a perfect April day. After Warren had left him Singleton had walked and thought for a long time.

The house felt empty now; for the first time since the early days of being alone he was conscious of its size and of the rooms that his daily cleaner kept dusted but which he never used.

His glass was half empty and he paused to refill it before stepping outside. The garden, which was large and rambling and surrounded the Victorian house, needed some work. Maybe after lunch, he told himself.

He lifted his drink, forced himself to sip, and he caught sounds of laughter from children in an adjoining garden and felt some sadness. It would have been better if they had had more. He made a mental note to call Ben that evening although he knew that at best the conversation would be polite formalities. He'd tried to tell Ben that he had felt about Debbie's death – and God he *had* felt – but that it was his personality coupled with his training that made him react to great shocks with apparent stoicism and mouthed platitudes. Ben had never believed, though; had never forgiven.

Was he living a similar lie now, even though he'd quit? What had Warren said when he had asked him why he should co-operate, literally risking his life?

"Because it just has to be tried, and if it is it needs someone like you. You've got the background, you've got the skills, but . . ."

"But," Singleton had said, "can be shown to be a disgruntled ex-employee, out working on his own now, and be thrown to the wolves if he gets caught."

Warren had not even bothered to answer.

"It's asking a lot, Cord."

"You want me to plead to your patriotism, remind you of why you signed on in the first place? Hell, you only quit because you didn't think we were doing our job well enough."

Singleton had thought Warren had finished, but the CIA Director had added gently, "And there's something else. Think how you'll feel about yourself if you turn it down. You're going to seed George, for all your talk. What are you? Forty-eight? Take a straight look in the mirror when you get home. Okay, it's nice not shaving and downing a half-pint of brandy down by the river before breakfast, but where are you going, George? You gonna drift through the rest of your life like some junkie?"

"I need time to think."

"There's not much time." And then, as he rose to return to the road, "You'll find a folder stashed under the seat in your car. It lays out some of the problems. Maybe you should read it before you decide."

"When do you need to know?"

"Six tonight. That gives you twelve hours. Long enough to decide whether you're in or out. I need to know fast."

"Okay." Singleton had not argued.

Now, with a little over five hours to go, he still didn't know. Why should he? The same question. If he succeeded, what were the rewards? Money? Nice, but he didn't need it. Praise? Who would ever know? His true role would never be known, not even locked away in those most secret of files. But he'd know. And from what Warren had hinted – referring to 'the highest authority' – so would the President.

And if he failed? Prison? Death? He turned and stared up

at the empty house. Maybe Warren was right; what had he to lose?

He looked down at his glass. Empty. Warren had been right about the drinking.

He decided.

He would read the papers anyway. Back inside, on impulse, he placed the steak back in the freezer, and mixed another drink, a weaker, longer one this time. Food could wait. Then he settled down to read.

In both the United States and the Soviet Union two small committees had been set up to monitor the situation, and they met all that Sunday.

Their tasks were not to initiate action, but to scrutinise reports of everything that was being done, and point out omissions or make suggestions for further avenues.

The American committee was the larger, but still consisted of only four men: an assistant attorney, a retired police chief, a long-term FBI agent and a representative from the CIA's anti-terrorist section.

None of the men knew anything of the significance of Ross. In monitoring developments they had been asked to concentrate on three problems: the search for the hijackers, names and locations of other terrorists who might possibly be seized and used as a bargaining weapon, and ways of establishing 'unofficial' US-hijacker contact.

The Russian committee was three strong and again, as the problems were seen to be ones of an investigative nature, they leaned towards detection: an investigator from the public prosecutor's office, an inspector from the Criminal Investigation Department and a ranking officer from the KGB's Counter Intelligence Department.

Like the Americans, they monitored the search, sought ways of establishing direct contact with the terrorists. But they also had a third brief: look for any evidence that linked the United States with the plot.

Material poured in from all over the world, names of possible candidates taken from computer files, transcripts of questioning of passengers and airport and airline staff, 'think' papers on the possible importance of the name the hijackers had chosen for a call-sign, details of interrogations of terrorists and their supporters rounded up in different countries . . .

Much of the information was shared; the bulk was common to both committees. But some information the United States and the Soviet Union retained for themselves.

The Americans remained quiet about their two main leads. The first concerned the jewellery the woman had worn. A fellow passenger, an insurance assessor, had been able to describe it in detail. Inquiries showed that two similar pieces had been stolen in Brussels fourteen months before.

The second was the detail that was emerging concerning the dead hijacker, Douglas Nash. The FBI had traced five raids on hospital records around the same date. One of them had been at the one where Nash was being treated.

The Russians in turn had a lead which they kept to themselves – the two jeeps left at the airstrip. They had been stolen.

Officially, the Algerian police were investigating and would pass on what they found to both sides. But unofficially the Algerians, heavily dependent on Soviet help, were being directed by the Russians.

The Soviet Union held another ace, but only Yury Voshchankin, the KGB head, and two other KGB men knew that. The FBI man on the American monitoring committee, Donald Sobers, was an 'agent in place', and was passing on everything he learned.

At five o'clock Singleton was still seated in the living room, papers around him on the carpet and a pad on his lap.

It was growing cool and he had still not eaten lunch, but he was too absorbed in the logistics of the problem to notice either cold or hunger.

The detail Warren had supplied was completely inadequate *if* Singleton went ahead. But it was more than enough for him to realise the problems and to work out what might be possible and what might be needed.

The prison in which the terrorists seized in January were held was in Northern Spain, north of Bilbao towards the coast, and completed only three years before.

Building had started in 1979, the year that the referendum on the future of the Basque country had been rejected by those who sought complete freedom and not the autonomy the Spanish government was prepared to offer them.

It had been built for two reasons: first, to satisfy those Basques who thought prisoners should be housed within the region itself (instead of in Soria, towards the south, as previously), and secondly with the intention of providing maximum security coupled with the maximum freedom within the walls that was possible in order to appease Basques and civil rights protesters generally.

It had been constructed in an area previously zoned for industrial development. The area around had been flattened for half a mile. At that point there were chain fences with sensitive devices buried underground.

The prison itself was surrounded with a wall twenty foot high, the top covered with barbed wire through which 2,300 volts of electricity passed. There were six watch towers. The flattened area was swept by lights and watched by closed circuit television.

In addition there was an infra-red barrier – anyone passing through the ray would sound an alarm – and dog patrols.

In contrast, within the prison there was some kind of freedom. Calculating that the prisoners could never get out, they were allowed to move comparatively freely.

This was made possible not only by the fantastic security outside but by the fact that most of the prison was built underground. The only parts above the surface were two exercise yards, a large one for 'normal' prisoners, a much smaller one for the more dangerous criminals. At present these were restricted to the terrorists.

The cells of these most dangerous inhabitants were underground, a thirty-yard passageway connecting them to the small yard.

Singleton noted all this carefully, studying the maps and the photographs of the surrounding countryside.

He would need a lot more, but suddenly, minutes away from six o'clock, he was satisfied.

On impulse, he went upstairs, shaved and changed. Then he dialled the number Warren had given him.

"Uncle Richard says he'd like to come to the party," he said.

He was sweating when he put down the receiver. But it was a relief. He would do it.

The next meeting was less than sixteen hours later.

This had also been specified in the light of Singleton agreeing.

Singleton drove his old Ford out on to the Beltway, took exit thirty-two and pulled into a parking lot at Landover Mall.

Warren was already there. Singleton changed cars, sliding into the passenger seat.

"I don't need to tell you how . . ."

"Can it, Cord. There's no need for speeches. Buy me dinner if we make it."

They talked for a half-hour. Mostly, it was Singleton, listing what he wanted in the way of further information, and what he expected he would want in equipment.

"Okay," said Warren at last. "No problems."

"I can give you your contact number now. It'll be manned twenty-four hours a day. All you do is say 'Is Mike on the way yet?' and leave the number you're at. I'll be back to that number exactly thirty minutes later. If the number you leave is engaged or there's no reply you'll be called at thirty minute intervals until you do reply.

"Once you fix things, we'll arrange other numbers abroad. Okay?"

"Okay."

Warren checked his watch. "You could make the noon flight to O'Hare," he said.

"I'll be on it."

Both knew time was their most precious commodity.

Singleton opened the door and began to slide out of Warren's car. Warren reached out, restrained him.

"One last thing, George, I forgot to say. There are twelve days yet. It may just be that we don't need you to go ahead – it might be sorted out some other way."

"So?"

"So, I mean don't go through with the operation unless you clear it with me. Wait for me to blow the whistle."

"When will I know?"

"Maybe not until the deadline day."

"And how do you tell me?"

Warren paused, and then began a faint smile. "I'll send you a message," he said. "If it's on you'll get the password.

"I'll tell you: 'Send in the Lions.'"

# 10

On North Michigan Avenue blustery winds swept a driving rain into the faces of pedestrians. But one thousand and three feet above them Andrew Muntwick could look out of his office windows at sunshine.

Muntwick had his headquarters – home and office, for they were intertwined – on the ninety-second floor of the John Hancock Center. Until he had moved in offices had been confined to the thirteenth to forty-first floors. By the expedient of buying the whole building he had taken over the top floor for his own use.

Only three elevators penetrated this far: one for staff, one for Muntwick's personal use and a third for the few visitors.

The staff lift was rarely used: three secretaries, nine security guards and five domestic staff, all had their own living quarters, and often did not leave the floor for days on end.

Muntwick's desk, behind which he sat at five twenty on the afternoon of 8 April, was precisely thirty feet long. He knew because he had had it built to that exact length. Behind it were six identical chairs, spaced an identical distance apart. In front of each chair was a pad, a silver pencil and a varying number of documents.

It was Muntwick's way of working, his six major current problems, all segregated, all waiting for his attention at the right moment.

This afternoon Muntwick was sitting at the extreme left of the desk studying a handwritten letter through a magnifying glass.

Occasionally he looked up and gazed through the window that almost reached from floor to ceiling. He liked the view best in winter: Lake Michigan covered in ice, perhaps an airplane passing beneath him, its shadow reflected. Today he looked down on clouds.

Every few seconds Muntwick moved the glass to a new word to study it. Occasionally he nodded. At last he was satisfied.

The man's writing confirmed what he had been told about Singleton. The upright script showed independence, the high crossing of the letter 't' confidence, the tightly closed 'a' and 'o' confirmed the man's ability to hold secrets and hide his true thoughts. Even the ugliness of the angular shaped letters pleased him, it showed that the man was incisive

Muntwick had found that men often lied, but their handwriting never. Nevertheless he reached under his desk and switched on his latest toy in readiness for Singleton's arrival, a lie detector that worked by measuring changes in a person's voice. Scientists at one of the Muntwick subsidiary companies claimed an eighty-five per cent reliability factor.

Muntwick was not sure that he believed in it a tenth as much as graphology, but with so much at stake he would use everything.

Muntwick reached into his waistcoat pocket for a gold fob watch and checked the time. Five thirty-seven. Singleton was due to arrive in eight minutes. Muntwick did not doubt his visitor would arrive precisely on time. His visitors did.

He placed the letter back on the desk, and opened a file that Warren had given him. The dossier inside was a dozen pages long, prepared especially for him. Singleton's credentials were impressive. He noted with satisfaction that Singleton was now divorced. He had never understood how a man could serve himself and someone else.

An orange light flashed on his desk – a sign that his visitor had arrived. But he continued to stare at the file. Let the man wait. It was not rudeness, nor an elementary desire to impress upon Singleton their relative status – Muntwick had long gone beyond such things. It was that the billionaire was used to the world revolving around him, and he felt he had earned that right.

What had Warren said of Singleton when he had flown in late the previous night? 'A casualty of our times.' Muntwick liked that. A man who believed so deeply – in his case about the basic evil of the Soviet Union and their intentions to the free world – that he could not adapt to his masters' changing stance. Muntwick shared Singleton's belief, but he knew you had to adapt. The Chinese, to his mind, were no better than the Russians, but he was working with them. He felt it was right he, Muntwick, should adapt. But he preferred rigidity like Singleton's in those he employed. Such men were easier to direct.

The light was still flashing, but no sound came from the intercom – the room was silent except when he ordained otherwise.

He leaned and pressed the nearest button that activated the microphones spaced around the room. "Tell Mr Singleton to come in."

Like Muntwick, Singleton had been reading, in his case the tycoon's file in the *Chicago Tribune* library during the hours he had to kill between his arrival in the city and his appointment.

He had also called a columnist friend in New York. But neither the files nor the conversation had yielded a great deal of information.

The only interview Muntwick appeared to have given had been to *Fortune* fourteen years before. Even that had been lacking in specifics and the article had been padded with details of Muntwick's early life, the best documented part of his career.

The clippings, Singleton noted, could have been divided into three phases. First there were the early ones that concentrated on a simple rags to riches, American boy makes good . . . the ten-year-old Muntwick forced to work part-time when his father was hospitalised and his mother unable to pay the bills, the teenage business man . . .

Then there was the middle period, when Muntwick had made it. These clippings were in the main antagonistic: Muntwick the despoiler of natural resources, Muntwick the symbol of American capitalist greed, the drugs that no one really needed, the forests destroyed for paper, the tankers that polluted, the low wages in Third World countries where he set up new plants . . .

Muntwick seemed to be everywhere; and everywhere he personified exploitation.

The third phase, dating roughly from the end of the Nixon Administration, treated him in a more neutral way. At this time he had been accorded the title 'the world's richest man'.

There were few items about the son – fewer, Singleton was told by his columnist friend, than there might have been had not Muntwick employed public relations advisers specifically to keep the boy's name out of the press. "Every so often it's said that the old man threatens to cut him off unless he toes the line," the columnist told Singleton.

"What happens?" Singleton had asked.

"Nothing," said the columnist. "The kid knows it's an idle threat. He knows that even the world's richest man gets to die sometime, and that it's no secret that he's the old man's bid for immortality. Nice relationship, isn't it? And crazy. You build that wealth, that empire, to leave to some shit kid that's not worth a cent."

No, neither the files nor the telephone call had helped much. But Singleton was conscious that they had achieved one thing: if later anyone probed they linked him to Muntwick. It was part of the deal: he was not only embarking on trying to rescue the terrorists in Spain, he was further disguising his real masters . . .

The girl behind the reception desk disturbed his thoughts. "You can go in now."

The double doors slid open as he neared them. He had not heard a telephone ring, a message relayed. He looked back. The girl wore what looked like a hearing aid, and he realised she must be continuously monitoring Muntwick's commands.

The doors led into an antechamber. A waiting guard searched Singleton, removed the Browning without surprise, commenting, "It'll be waiting when you leave."

The guard pressed a button, muttered a number that Singleton could not catch, and more doors slid open.

Singleton stepped forward on to deep purple carpet. His eyes did not take in the rest of the furnishings – Muntwick himself was too much of a surprise. The latest photograph in the *Chicago Tribune* morgue had showed a middle aged man on board a yacht, out of focus, clutching a glass and with his arm around a girl. It was not a good picture and probably twenty years old, but it was the most recent and seemingly was used everytime newspapers wanted to publish a piece on Muntwick.

The man in front of Singleton was thinner, gaunt almost, and looked a very old man. When he stood to greet his visitor, which he did with old world courtesy, Singleton noted he was tall: very tall.

The billionaire led him away from the desk to some easy chairs. Singleton knew of the throat operation but was unprepared for the voice. It rasped, sounding separated from the body that produced it, like a piece of bad dubbing.

"I don't know if you smoke, Mr Singleton, but if you do normally I'd rather you didn't. It affects my throat." He pointed towards his chest.

"I don't and I'd be surprised if you didn't know that, Mr Muntwick. In fact I'd be surprised if you don't know what size shoes I wear and what I ate for breakfast. I'd say you were that kind of man."

Muntwick laughed – a strange gurgling sound. He stood and poured a cup of coffee from a bubbling machine. "I thought perhaps you'd like a coffee, Mr Singleton. No sugar, I understand."

He fetched himself a glass of mineral water and eased himself into a comfortable chair. "I understand," he said, "that you've a crazy idea that might interest me."

"It might. I tried official sources first, but they're too scared. They warned me off."

"Tell me."

Singleton looked around the room theatrically.

Muntwick noted, understood, and commented: "It's safe. Only two people including me have access to this room. The very occasional visitor like you is searched. Nevertheless, this room will be checked when you leave. It's safe to talk, I assure you."

Singleton sipped his coffee, looked in vain for somewhere to place the cup, and began. "As you know, it's the hijacking. My reading is that no matter what the pressures neither the President nor the Soviets are going to give way. In the case of the President I doubt if the country would let him anyway. We're all sick of being pushed around. Our macho's at stake – and, forgive me being blunt, apart from that no one cares too much about the terrorists' prisoners. Volkov – well, he's a Soviet; Miss North – we'll cry a few crocodile tears but really we're enjoying the excitement; your son . . ."

He paused in case Muntwick wanted to say anything but there was silence.

"What I propose is that we cut all the red tape, get right to the heart of the problem. I understand that you read a lot of ancient history, Mr Muntwick. I see the problem like the Gordian knot. Others are trying to find a way of untying it. I'd like to cut it."

"So how do you propose to do this, Mr Singleton?" Warren, transparently nervous, had told Muntwick little beyond the fact that Singleton had, unsuccessfully, approached the Administration with a totally unacceptable idea that might nevertheless intrigue him.

He did not find it strange that the CIA Director should tell him this. Such men's jobs never lasted long. He imagined that Warren was already contemplating the future and wondering about the possibilities of joining the Muntwick organisation.

"My proposition, Mr Muntwick, is that we concentrate on the hijackers' key demand – the release of the international band of terrorists captured in January and now held in Spain. That's what they really want. I reckon that if we gave them that and the money they want, we could get your son back."

"How'd you give them the terrorist prisoners if the governments won't play?"

"That's where I'd cut the knot. I'd blast them out of prison – after, that is, doing a deal with the hijackers."

Muntwick did not ask whether Singleton could do that. Obviously he believed he could, or he would not have been there.

"And the money?"

"By your standards it's not a lot of money, Mr Muntwick. I guess Miss North's studio and the Frenchman's family would put up some cash, but I'd like to keep them out. If we did something like I propose, it would have to be kept a real tight operation."

Muntwick rose, walked to his desk, and slid open a drawer revealing a console of buttons. He pressed a combination of them. "Come," he said. "I'd like to show you something."

He led Singleton to some doors at one end of the room. They opened, and there was an antechamber and a guard and then another set of sliding doors.

Muntwick led the way through these and the doors closed behind them. There was total silence.

The room was rectangular, about sixty feet long, artificially lit, and the walls were covered with icons.

"I come in here when I want to experience real beauty, when I want to think, to meditate on the timelessness of man."

He took Singleton's arm and led him further into the room. "Do you know anything about icons, Mr Singleton?"

"I know they sell for a lot of money."

Muntwick shrugged. "That's immaterial. Many of the ones you see today are rubbish. Three hundred years ago the quality began to decline. Here you will see nothing later than the sixteenth century."

He paused in front of one. "This is the Virgin and St John at the foot of the cross. A Rublyov, Mr Singleton. One of the masterpieces of the world. Literally beyond any price."

He stood back and waved around the room. "These are the possessions I treasure above all. Seen by no eyes except mine. Worth a small kingdom."

He stared down at Westland, his eyes piercing.

"But I would give them all for my son, Mr Singleton. You understand? You understand?" The rasp of his voice echoed in the still room.

"So do what you suggest. Spend whatever it takes. Pay whatever it costs. But get my son."

# 11

The Algerian, whose name was Mourad Khelif, broke easily.

The two policemen had taken him early that afternoon from the interrogation room to the villa among the trees high in the hills overlooking Algiers.

They gagged him, stripped him and strapped him face upwards on a table. The elder one, who twenty-five years before had been tortured in a similar way by the French, clipped on the electrodes to a finger and a toe and turned on the magneto.

Khelif resisted the first shocks. The policeman moved the one from his foot, attached it to an ear lobe, and turned the magneto higher.

The man's body arched and shook and there was a crack as his front teeth shattered. Nevertheless, the policeman moved his hand as though to operate the machine again.

"Enough. He'll talk." The words, spoken in perfect dialectal Algerian Arabic, came from a man whose documentation said he was Iranian, but who's real name was Yakov Gozori. He leaned in the doorway of the deserted house – it was due for demolition and redevelopment – arm drooped against the door-jamb, looking on unconcerned as though watching a normal domestic scene.

In truth, though, he did not like physical torture. Mostly it was unnecessary – which was one of the key words in his vocabulary. It was also outmoded, which was another. But he had to concede, it was effective this time. And of course, he thought, it was the only thing these Algerian barbarians knew. In reality it did not matter they were Algerian, his hatred was a result of the years he had had to live under deep cover in the country. He would have felt the same about the native population wherever he was.

Neither his face nor voice betrayed his emotions, however. "Untie him. Bring him in here."

Gozori moved into the adjoining room to wait. He had hastily arranged it before the two Algerian policemen and their prisoner had arrived. Some furniture, not worth taking, remained in the house; he had furnished the room with a table and one chair. The blinds at the window were closed.

There was a packet of small cheroots on the table, and he lit one from the stub already in his hand. Like many Russians he chain-smoked. After living the lie of deep cover almost twice as long as was usually considered desirable, his hands had begun to shake with strain and too much drink. He was forty-six, but looked in his mid-fifties, and had started to develop bouts of depression that neither alcohol nor drugs would lift.

Nevertheless he remained good at his job, although his work was more closely monitored these days. "Two more years," they had argued to themselves at Moscow Centre. They did so because he would be difficult to replace – because he had been brought up in the Central Asian Republic of Tadzhikskaya, he passed easily for Iranian.

At the same time, because his mother – who came from Georgia – has passed on a touch of the swarthy Mediterranean-type looks, he could at a pinch pass himself off as an Algerian.

The Algerian prisoner was dragged through the doorway, still naked and whimpering. The policemen threw him to the floor and stood over him until Gozori beckoned to them to leave.

There were two glasses on the table, a jug of water and a bottle of anisette. Gozori filled a glass, gestured the Algerian to rise and handed it to him.

Khelif had difficulty holding the glass.

"Drink!" Gozori did not care whether the man was an

abstaining Moslem; no one would refuse at a time like this.

The Algerian tried, but liquid spilled out of the corner of his mouth joining the blood that already ran there.

"All of it."

The Algerian used both hands. His body still choked with sobs. Much of the liquid ran over his body, but at last the glass was empty.

The Russian took the receptacle from him and then poured himself a drink.

"Now talk," he said. The Algerian's eyes darted to the blinds. Gozori could read the man's mind, he was wondering whether he was not a softer touch than the two who had tortured him.

"Or," Gozori continued in the same even tone, "I'll give you back to them and let them play all they like." He smiled. "They like it, you know. One was tortured by the French, and nearly died. He's been strange ever since.

"He's a real specialist, can make it last for days. Long before the end you are praying for death . . ."

Finding the Algerian had been a lucky piece of detection. Having him seized and questioned by two men who were in his direct pay was incredible luck. The information would have been passed to the Russians in any event, of course, but so many would have been aware of it that it could have hardly failed to get to the Americans sooner or later.

Khelif, a well-known minor thief, had fitted the description of a man seen looking suspicious some two weeks before near the oil refinery at El Harrach, an industrial town just outside Algiers. One of the jeeps abandoned at the airstrip had, police knew, been stolen from the parking lot of a chemical plant in the same town.

Picked up and taken to police headquarters by the two policemen, Khelif had rapidly confessed to stealing the jeep in El Harrach, but had insisted that he had then abandoned it quickly after using it to transport some goods.

That was when Gozori had been called, and Khelif had been moved quietly and quickly to the villa in the hills.

The story emerged as Gozori chain-smoked his cheroots,

sucking the acrid smoke deep into his lungs, and drinking glass after glass of anisette.

It was four hours before he was satisfied that he had been told everything. The story was straightforward. Khelif had been approached by a man he knew only as Amir, who, at a second meeting, had introduced a European. Fortunately Khelif, like most criminals, had a trained memory and his description of the man was good.

The European wanted Khelif to supply two vehicles, preferably jeeps, probably in seventy-two hours time, but he would receive instructions later, including where to deliver them.

This Khelif had duly done. But there was more, and it was here that Gozori became most interested.

After supplying the jeeps, both of which he left in designated parking lots in Algiers, he was asked if he would carry out one further assignment: pick up an abandoned Fiat at Dellys, a town along the coast, two days hence.

He was then to drive it the five hundred kilometres to Tlemcen where it had been rented from a car hire agency, leave it outside during the night, and push the keys through the door.

After that he was to make his way back to Algiers by train and forget everything that had happened. For his work he had received the equivalent of five thousand dollars.

Satisfied at last, Gozori stood wearily, stretched and opened the door.

The two policemen were seated, playing cards, drinking Kronenbourg beer from the bottle. They rose as Gozori entered.

"I'm leaving now," he said. "You're not to talk about this. Nothing has taken place. You made a mistake with your prisoner. When you found out you freed him."

The elder policeman looked towards the room Gozori had just left. "What about him?"

Gozori deliberated quickly. Was there much more to be extracted? There was always something, but he doubted whether there was much. Should he show Khelif photographs? Possibly, but it was marginal: the description the petty crook had given was so detailed. Under normal conditions, the answer would have been Yes. But the important thing here was that Khelif should not talk to anyone else.

Too risky to keep him around.

"Get rid of him," he said.

As he closed the front door and made for the path through the trees he heard the muffled screams begin.

# 12

Even though he had not eaten at all during the day Singleton was not hungry. Nevertheless, when the tray of nuts arrived with the drink he finished them within minutes and asked for more, nervousness rather than hunger.

It was seven thirty p.m., ninety minutes after he had left Muntwick, and two and a half hours before the take-off of the plane he had planned to take to Paris.

In the cab from the Hancock Building, though, he had changed his mind; the flight he was now on was not heading for France, it was returning him to Washington.

As he sipped at his bourbon, forcing himself not to gulp, he began trying to persuade himself that his change of plan would not make any difference, he would rise soon after five, make his vital telephone calls then, catch the nine a.m. Concorde to de Gaulle and be there late afternoon local time.

But he knew, difference or not, he would have done what he had; after four years he had to see her again. It was partly superstition – it had always been before an assignment; seeing her not only made him seem fully alive, but – like touching a lucky talisman – gave him some protection. Even more so, it was the realisation that there was little else left – if he died this time, who would truly mourn him? His ex-wife? He thought she would remember him with fondness. But mourn? He doubted it.

It was a marriage from which he had taken more than he had given, or could give. As an employee, albeit a secretary, of the agency she should have known what it was like, but she had never – before their marriage – imagined it transferred to her *home* life.

The little things, the big things. Not being able to talk – apart from occasional hints when they were vitally necessary it was best she knew as little as possible. When he was working under embassy cover there was the unvoiced but clear puzzlement and sometimes patronising tones of the wives of colleagues whose husbands gained promotion while he stood still, not knowing that his FSO ranking was a fiction and no more. The telephone calls in the middle of the night which he answered like a doctor on house call. The days away from home to unspecified places from which he might or might not return.

The plane landed a few minutes ahead of time, a fact that gave him unmerited relief, a sign that he had done the right thing, and one reinforced when he stepped straight into a cab.

The driver took the address, barely glancing at him. Singleton was long reconciled to the fact that he looked ordinary; it was, in truth, one of the qualities that had made him so good an agent. In such a role it was best to be anonymous. Singleton had always prided himself that he could meet someone two, three, even four times, and each time the other would think it was the first.

Kate hadn't thought that. Maybe that was what had made it so special. That and, of course, the circumstances.

The cab passed St Thomas Circus and turned right on to Rhode Island Avenue. It was nine thirty-five and Singleton knew he should telephone: she might be out, she might be with another man. She might even be married, but he doubted that: that was one piece of news, he thought, he would have heard.

When they had first met she had been living in McLean. A year after her husband's death she had moved to Brookland where she lived now. Singleton had been dubious, but she had settled well into what was one of the few blue-collar neighbourhoods with a good sized white population left in the inner city. She taught elementary school; as far as he knew, she still did.

The street, as the cab pulled to a halt, was quiet and much as Singleton remembered it. The house had been newly painted. There were two bell-pushes; Kate rented out the top floor.

He pushed one, suddenly conscious of the case at his feet – even in the past, when his visits had almost always been before leaving Washington, he had not been so blatant.

The nervousness that he had felt in the plane but forgotten in the cab returned. He dusted the lapels of his coat, smoothed his hair with his hand.

The door was opened on a chain. "Who is it? What do you want?"

There was no mistaking the voice; deep, husky, slightly breathless, a voice that, he knew, made other women immediately suspicious. It dated back to a childhood ailment of the vocal chords, a fact Kate often found herself volunteering defensively to wives of men she met.

"George," he said. "Me. George." He had worked out elaborate sentences, but they were forgotten. After four years he was like a tongue-tied adolescent.

She hesitated a few moments, slipped the chain and opened the door wide, not moving. She was wearing slacks and a shirt, her hair was tucked up in a bun (it had been short when he had last seen her) and she wore no make-up.

"You pick your time," she said, standing aside. "Four years and you can't even choose a moment when I'm looking glamorous."

Then she reached out, took his hand, and drew him inside.

"Come on in," she said. "I'll fix you a drink."

It was five minutes after three, and apart from the light bounced by the lamps of the occasional passing car the room was in darkness.

Singleton could feel her, still curled up against him naked, and he could smell the potent mixture of sweat, sex and the

Southern Comfort which they had brought to bed with them, well after midnight and still nervous with each other.

Singleton had set his wrist watch alarm for four forty-five but he was already wide awake. He had fallen asleep minutes after they had made love, relieved and pleased it had still been so good after all this while, and conscious that she was still awake and holding him.

He reached for the bedside table, fingers groping in the dark until he found the glass. He manoeuvred it to his lips, tilted it, realised it was still half full, and sipped the strong sweetness.

Her body was deep under the covers, her head level with his chest, the way it always used to be. She murmured and turned and her stomach brushed his thigh.

How many times over the years had they made love? He could, he supposed, have counted them accurately, but that would have meant linking them with assignments, which he did not want to do. But certainly no more than a dozen.

It was a strange relationship, and had been from the start, yet they had found something within each other for which both of them hungered.

Kate Galbraith's husband, Teddy, had been one of Singleton's colleagues – not a close one, just someone he had passed a few times in the corridor or shared a table with in the company dining room when they were both at base.

They'd both found themselves in the Lebanon in 1976, though. Singleton had been angling for a variety of short-term assignments in the year since Debbie had died. He hadn't got over it – it wasn't a disease that normally killed kids; his friends tried to console him that, in his place, they wouldn't have rushed home either.

There had been a meeting with a Moslem who had been feeding good information; Singleton met him together with Galbraith and an Israeli intelligence officer.

What no one had bargained for was that the man was mad; he had pulled the pin on a grenade in front of them. Galbraith had died diving for him; the Israeli had been blinded. Singleton, thanks to the cushion provided by Galbraith's body, escaped with one slight scratch over the left eye and a partial deafness which disappeared without treatment within two weeks.

Galbraith, like Singleton listed as a State Department employee, was flown back to Washington. To all intents and purposes, though, he had never left the country; the story – even for his wife – was he had died in a fire while attending a seminar near San Diego.

Despite the fact that Galbraith had saved his life, Singleton doubted whether he would have done anything were it not for Debbie's death. He persuaded himself that Galbraith's wife, in her grief, might reconcile herself better if she knew her husband had died for something – even if it were for someone she didn't know.

Against all the rules, he had called on her, long after darkness because some of her neighbours were company men too and one might have recognised him.

She gave no indication whether she felt helped by his visit and what he told her, but she thanked him gracefully, and said she hoped he would call again. He did. But it was not until after she moved to Brookland that they made love. And then it became a strange, irregular but defined pattern; he called when he was about to leave on an assignment, and she was always alone when he arrived. He never knew whether she had cancelled an appointment, even sent someone away. They talked a great deal but about small things, and there was always a hint in the way she behaved that she never knew whether he would return again. Hours later he left and whether she was asleep or not she always acted as though she was.

Three forty by the luminous hands on his watch. The glass was empty. Singleton wanted another drink.

He eased himself out of the bed and quietly, so as not to wake her, made for the door. He collided with a chest of drawers and cursed, but Kate's breathing did not change.

There was a long towelling robe in the bathroom and he slipped it on before walking along the passageway to the living room. The drinks were on a tray near the window and he poured a large scotch before beginning to prowl the room in his restlessness.

It was an oddly impersonal room, almost as though she had discarded the clutter of oddments that constitute part of most people's past. There was only one photograph, and that not of Teddy. He thought it was of her parents, although they had aged a lot since the last photograph he had seen.

The most revealing thing was the piles of books, magazines and newspapers – a glance took in Tolstoy and Harold Robbins, *The National Review* and *Readers Digest*, a movie monthly and a travel magazine. She was, he recalled with a smile, a woman who read anything and everything, totally indiscriminately, the act of reading being enough in itself. "My escape," she'd said once. "Expensive, but cheaper than drink or pot."

He paused at a heap of newspapers – the *St Petersburg, Florida, Times*, and then remembered that it was her home town, and that she'd told him that her parents always kept up a subscription for her, apparently convinced that while there was such a tie she might return to live there one day.

And wasn't there something personal, she had once told him? A journalist on the paper, someone she'd grown up with, someone whom her parents thought she might marry? Leger, Ralph Leger. That was the name. He remembered it because the reporter had won a Pulitzer the year before for a series on the misuse of medical data banks.

He had closed the door behind him and he heard it open now. Kate came inside, her hair down, her eyes blinking in half-sleep. She wore his shirt. Even without shoes, she was as tall as him, around five foot nine inches, and the edge finished an inch above the dark of her pubic hair.

"You look like someone who's been laid," said Singleton.

She disregarded the remark, found cigarettes, lit one, and said, "It's only just four. You said five. You haven't started lying to me?"

He realised that many of the times when he had left, believing she was asleep, she must have been lying, eyes closed, pretending.

"I couldn't sleep." He shrugged his free hand and lifted his glass and sipped. "And I guess I felt the need for a drink. I'm getting old, Kate. I'm going over the top."

They had never talked about what he did or what her husband had done. It was always there but left unspoken. But now, she asked, "You're back? You didn't quit at all?"

"No, I did quit. That was real." He waited for her to react but she remained silent.

It was against his training, his personality, the life he had led for twenty-one years, but he had to say something.

"This is just one last one. Something I have to do."

She ground out her cigarette. "For the past? For money? For excitement? For ideals?"

He poured more whisky and sipped it neat, visibly pondering her question.

"For ideals, I think," he said at last. "And I suppose a bit for the past, to prove I can."

She took the glass from him and took his hand. "Come back to bed," she said. "We've an hour yet."

At five fifteen when he arose she did not stir. Nor did she two hours later, when after his series of transatlantic telephone calls he kissed her cheek and left for the waiting cab.

Gozori stumbled off the overnight train from Algiers, awake but still hung-over from the scotch and the sleeping tablets.

Despite that, though, he was pleased to have slept, sleeping had been difficult in recent months.

Tlemcen, near the Western frontier of Algeria, was his – and everyone's – favourite city in the country: domes and minarets, crenellated ramparts, crowded suqs with sandal makers, weavers, coppersmiths . . . Of all Algerian cities, it was the most Arabic – straight out of *The Arabian Nights*.

Gozori breakfasted at a pavement café before making his way to the car rental office which was in a side street off the Avenue Commandant Faredj.

Inside, there were two men, one busy with a customer. To the other Gozori showed a security police pass, and was immediately swept through into a small rear office and given mint tea.

There was a few minutes of polite talk before the car rental manager asked, "I can be of assistance?"

Gozori sipped his tea and nodded. "You rented out a Fiat, registration 294164Z. It was returned overnight 29 March, parked outside. I would like to see the documents of rental."

"What's wrong? There were no marks of an accident."

"Security. Let me see the papers."

The manager sorted through a grey filing cabinet, and Gozori was pleased that the Algerians had inherited the French passion for bureaucracy. Everything was there.

The name of the renter was given as Georges Heidweiller. The address was that of an apartment block in Algiers, and Gozori had no doubt it would prove to be false.

His eyes scanned the form: "Nationality: Dutch. Passport Number . . ."

There was no entry in the space marked 'Credit Card'.

"He paid cash?"

The manager took back the form, studied it, and said, "Yes. He is entitled to a small refund. I don't know if we have sent it yet."

"Describe him for me, please?"

"We have so many customers." Nevertheless, the description was close to the one given by Khelif.

"Did he say where he was going?"

"Only that he wanted to tour."

"What language did he speak?"

"French."

There was a something in the manager's tone, and Gozori prompted, "And . . . ?"

"It may be nothing, but it did not sound like the French of a Dutchman. It was too good. Oh, he could have been a good linguist, but it was too . . . too French,"

"Idiomatic?"

"Yes. That is the word."

Gozori began to fold the rental agreement to put it into his pocket. "Is this the only copy?"

"One more." The manager began to realise what was happening.

"Fetch it."

The manager did so, and Gozori took it from him. "You never saw this man. You never rented him a car. You understand me?"

He noted the look of fear.

"Now I'd like to see the car if it is here." It was.

The plane was a twelve-seater Beechcraft but Singleton was the only passenger. It had been waiting for him when he arrived at Charles de Gaulle Airport, and barely an hour after take-off it was coming in to land at Clermont Ferrand.

He had paid for the private charter with a credit card, barely bothering to listen to the scale of charges; in the end Muntwick would pay.

The flight, first the Concorde from Washington and then the short hop south from Paris, had given him all the time he needed to think and to plan.

Concorde had been only two-thirds full and he had made notes without fear of being overlooked. He had set things down on paper to help his thoughts, destroying the notes before he settled and tried to doze.

He had listed the equipment he needed; Warren already had that in hand. Then the men he needed to see: three only if it worked well, two to help, one to establish contact with the hijackers.

He was on the way to see one of them. Seeing them singly though would burn up three precious days. And if they weren't contactable quickly? He had reserves, but he pushed the thought from his mind.

At best, then, he had realised, eight days to actually handle the operation, after which he would almost certainly need to return to the States. Could it be done? The others could carry on with their roles while he was away.

Finally, satisfied that it could – and with, if necessary, two days to spare if there were problems – he had torn the paper into small bits, pulped them in the washbasin and flushed the remains down the lavatory.

Only then did he allow himself to think of Kate, but only briefly – to dwell on the memory was dangerous.

A nondescript-looking Peugeot was waiting for him at the airport at Clermont. The driver, who Singleton knew was an ex-Foreign Legionnaire and Farrell's resident chauffeur/bodyguard, talked little on the journey.

Rush hour was over and they were soon out of the built-up area. The chauffeur drove fast, with concentration, through the wooded hills and after half an hour they reached the lakes and the tall blue fir trees.

The house, built in a clearing, overlooked one of the lakes, and was reached by a long narrow track, Farrell was waiting when the car pulled to a halt.

It had been three years since Singleton had seen him, but he had not changed. He was short, stocky, with a wide face, and a mass of black curly hair. His nose was crooked where it had been broken and reset badly.

Both he and Singleton were the same age, forty-eight, but the Irish-American could have been in his mid-thirties. His face had a boyish look, unlined, as though he had lived a life untouched by fear, stress or danger.

That, Singleton knew, could not have been further from the truth. Singleton had met him in the mid-sixties in Vietnam. Farrell already had a failed marriage, a failed air ferry business and a failed attempt to kick the bottle behind him.

He had been one of a band attracted to Vietnam to escape their problems. There he had been drawn into CIA work, and had also begun his career as a smuggler, one which he had continued and refined after fleeing Vietnam in ultimate disgust after watching a friendly village 'dusted' on a lieutenant's whim.

His smuggling business had since become a small empire, directed from offices in Zurich, Paris and Berlin. He moved gold into France, Spain, Italy, Turkey, Morocco; diamonds anywhere for a percentage of the value, taking all risks including that of compensation if they were seized; people across frontiers . . .

Farrell greeted Singleton warmly and led him around the house into a small, enclosed garden edging on to the lake.

It was almost dark and Farrell lit a ship's hurricane lantern hanging from a pole above a small plank table. On the table bottles of beer lay in a bath of melting ice. Without asking Farrell removed a bottle, flipped off the cap and handed it to Singleton with a glass.

Singleton had not been to the house before, had not known it existed, until he had made his telephone calls.

"You had a job finding me," said Farrell. "I'm sorry. This is my hideaway. Not many people come here."

His voice retained a faint Irish accent. His words were spoken softly but the implication was clear: he hoped Singleton had a good reason for disturbing him.

Singleton drank the beer quickly and reached for another. "May I?"

"Sure. Go ahead."

There was a noise behind them. Singleton turned and saw a dark-haired woman, in her early twenties, very small and petite in a long white dress. She held a plate of hors d'oeuvres which she set on the table.

She took Farrell's arm with both hands and squeezed.

"Martine," said Farrell. "My wife." He spoke to her in French, and then said to Singleton, "She speaks very little English. I've just told her you are an old friend."

Singleton nodded. He spoke French too, but it was not in his nature to volunteer anything. You never knew when it might be useful.

Martine returned to the house. "I didn't know you were married," said Singleton. "Sorry. I would have written."

"I am – and we're not," Farrell said. He smiled at Singleton's puzzlement. "I was married a long time ago," he explained. "She's still in the States. Good Catholics that we are, we don't get divorced. I don't mind. She doesn't ask for much. Martine lives here. The local people think we're married, and that it's a shame I have to travel so much. But she has her parents near." He pointed into the trees. "I built them a house up there. They seem happy with the set-up."

He poured himself another beer and reached for a canapé. For such a stocky man his movements were incredibly delicate. Singleton remembered the gentle ease with which he had once watched him drop his helicopter into a clearing with the air still and windless, the worst kind for a helicopter pilot, chatting softly as automatic fire burst all around . . .

"I take it you'll be staying for dinner – Martine's a good cook. And we've a guest room."

"If you still want me around when I've told you why I'm here."

"I must admit I'd been wondering that."

Singleton explained in the briefest terms, laying stress on the fact that he was working for Muntwick.

"Why me? And why should I be interested?"

Singleton could have stressed the money; no matter how wealthy a man was, who could not use an extra million dollars?

But he did not, because that was no way to hook Farrell. "Because," he said slowly, "I need the best damned helicopter pilot in the whole world."

They talked well into the night and again the following morning before Singleton left for the airport at Clermont.

It was not until the last minute that Farrell formally agreed to get involved – but it was clear almost from the beginning that he was hooked.

Like Singleton he liked the problem, and the idea of involvement. As his smuggling empire had grown he had become increasingly divorced from actual operations. Much of the time he operated like a perfectly reputable and boring businessman, producing estimates, lunching prospective clients.

Studying details of the prison, he quickly saw why Singleton needed a helicopter – it was the only chance. Even then there were risks. One watch tower needed to be put out of action; ideally, there needed to be diversions within the prison. The essence, though, was speed, and the skill of the pilot.

They discussed an even more immediate problem than the break-in itself – getting a helicopter in or into Spain.

"There are no more than four private ones in the whole country," Farrell said, stating something Singleton had already checked. "And they're closely watched and controlled. We'd need to take one in."

Singleton had already thought this through, but he remained silent, letting Farrell involve himself more and more.

Finally, it was agreed. Farrell looked up from his morning coffee cup, eyes grinning despite the tiredness. "By Jesus," he said, "I think we could do it."

"I think so too."

"How many more men?"

"I'd like to keep it down to one more. He'd have to double up. The tighter the better."

Farrell whistled. "He'd have to be good."

"I was thinking of Kemp," said Singleton.

# 13

The house stood alone, high on the South Downs, some fifty miles from London.

It was built of stone against the wind, as were the high walls that enclosed a long garden.

"You want me to stay?" asked the taxi driver who had brought Singleton the three-mile drive from the village.

"No. If he's not in I'll wait." The village postman had told Singleton that he had seen Kemp that morning.

Singleton checked his watch: almost twelve thirty. He stood at the gateway until the taxi was out of sight, enjoying the same kind of quiet stillness that he had experienced only six and a half hours before on leaving Farrell.

He had left his suitcase at the Left Luggage Office at Victoria Station in London. He walked up the path, breathing in the smell of wild flowers, raised his hand to ring the bell and noticed that the door was open.

He pushed it and it swung back. There was a long hallway, dark, wide and cool, the walls decorated with ancient weapons. He tried the first two doors: the rooms were empty.

The third, at the end of the passageway, was in almost total darkness, but Singleton entered and closed the door behind him. Kemp was in one corner, naked except for a pair of briefs. He was standing on his head, his eyes closed.

Singleton was not a fat man, but Kemp's body seemed not to contain a spare ounce of flesh. Singleton could make out the line of the ribs, the shape of the diaphragm, the curves of the shoulder bones.

Without opening his eyes Kemp said, "Don't stand in the

doorway, George. Come in. Don't mind me. I think better this way."

Singleton closed the door and stood waiting. Since they had last met Kemp had grown a beard which was flecked with red and grey.

"You knew I was coming?"

"They telephoned me from the village. Described you. They respect my privacy."

There was a sudden rustling sound to Singleton's right and he turned nervously, instinctively raising his right hand.

"Easy, George, easy," said Kemp, opening his eyes and swinging down to his feet. "He won't hurt you. He just likes sitting here with me, but sudden movements make him nervous."

Singleton's eyes were still fixed on the cruel eyes that gleamed out of the shadows – a huge eagle set on a perch.

He stepped backwards and out of the corner of his eye saw Kemp reaching out for clothes draped across a chair and sliding on denim trousers and a track suit top.

The eagle remained on the perch. Singleton could not make out whether it was chained – but its head was flicked in Singleton's direction and he was conscious of the bird's talons.

Kemp went to a shelf, took something and walked over to the eagle, hand outstretched, his mouth making soft noises. The bird's beak opened, and Singleton realised that Kemp had given it a hunk of raw meat.

"Come on," said Kemp, opening the door. "I want you to see something beautiful." Singleton followed, glad to be out of the room, and then amused when he realised what Kemp had said: was it really only two days since Muntwick had come out with a similar phrase?

They left the house by a rear door and entered the walled garden. It was silent and still. Then Singleton realised it was full of tall wooden perches, spaced several yards apart in a huge circle.

On each perch, its head encased in a hood which covered the eyes, was a great bird of prey. All the birds were tethered to their posts by a light chain and a narrow band of metal circling one leg.

The birds were motionless in the dark of their hoods, but alert.

Kemp pulled on a hawking glove, and took one bird, a peregrine falcon, from its perch, removing the hood.

He stroked it and the crazed eyes became still.

Not talking, Kemp led the way outside and in fifteen minutes they were standing silent on the Downs, Kemp's eyes scanning the sky.

"It's been a long time, George," he said. "What do you want?"

Singleton remained quiet, his eyes drawn by the cruel head of the bird, and his mind remembering Kemp's past and registering the stifled aggression within the man.

Kemp, like Farrell, had been drawn into the fringes of intelligence, but in his case for the British. Originally he had followed his father into the army, but could not bear the regimentation and had left and entered journalism.

It was here that he had been recruited as a part-time helper by the Secret Intelligence Service, benefiting from the quiet help they were able to give him in his work from time to time, and also, he had to admit, getting a silent thrill from being an insider in such a tiny club.

He had always been drawn to Africa and he had always been a loner; two things the Service quite liked and had taken advantage of. At the age of thirty-three though, something had happened which even later, with the picture incredibly clear, he could hardly believe: the SIS, faced with a key man being arrested in an African State, had sought to divert attention for a short, crucial time by the crude but effective means of providing a diversion – Kemp. He had been arrested, tortured, then turned loose finally only after appeals from the United Nations.

The Service had been sympathetic. But Kemp knew. His limp reminded him always.

He continued working for the SIS, albeit in very minor roles. His chance had come two years later, at the age of thirty-five. A minor African dictator, facing overthrow, needed instant cash to bribe enough army officers necessary to keep him in power. The British Government, who wanted the same thing, supplied the money, in Swiss francs. And Kemp was the courier

Reading the situation correctly – the dictator was beheaded two months later – he removed the equivalent of $140,000 before delivery.

Soon afterwards he had quit journalism, bought the old farmhouse, and settled down to breeding and hunting birds of prey, a sport that he had first become excited about on a trip to Saudi Arabia nine years before.

Singleton realised that Kemp was still awaiting his answer. "I'm out," he said. "You know that?"

"I know what I've heard. I stopped believing a long time ago."

Singleton disregarded the answer. "I've a freelance assignment. I need some help."

"Shhhh . . ."

Kemp was staring into the pale blue afternoon sky. A rook flew high overhead.

Kemp extended his arm and the falcon soared upwards, far above the rook, hovered and then began its dive.

"We call it the stoop," said Kemp quietly, his eyes fixed upon the scene.

"Fastest creature in the world, they say," said Singleton. "Maybe reaches a hundred miles an hour."

Kemp switched his eyes to Singleton's face, but the American was looking upwards, impassive.

The hawk struck the rook, a scene that made Singleton shudder, but which, he had to admit, had a sad and terrible beauty.

He turned to look at Kemp's face. It carried a look of great intensity.

"A perfect killing machine," he said. "It's not cruel because that's what they were made for. Just that. Do you know, George, that man was flying birds of prey before he even learned to write?"

There was a sudden beat of wings and the falcon settled back on Kemp's glove.

The man began to walk and without any change of tone in his voice, he said, "What do you want, George? Why have you come?"

"I told you. I've a freelance assignment."

"Why me? I'm out. I've been out a long time. You know that."

"Farrell's in."

Kemp stopped and turned to face him, and Singleton was conscious of the bird only feet from his face.

"It must be a big one. He doesn't need the money. I take it there is money. It isn't one of those for old times' sake jobs. . . ?"

Singleton disregarded the bitterness. "I need someone who can drive a truck and who can shoot well."

"Why should I risk it? You've seen what I've got." He was reacting just as Farrell had. But here the bait was money.

"I understand it's an expensive sport," he said gently. No need to remind Kemp that he had carried out the occasional assignment for Farrell – the money he had stolen must be low by now.

"Just think what you could do with a really immense amount of money." He forced himself to look away from the bird and into Kemp's eyes.

"Like say . . . one million pounds."

Karen Huisman sat at the plastic-topped kitchen table and finished writing the letter to her parents.

It would be posted from Switzerland, where she was supposedly holidaying with friends, and she included a colour photograph of herself against a background of Swiss peaks – taken some weeks before for just this purpose.

The house, in the outskirts of Liège, Belgium, near the German border, was a long way from where she was supposed to be. But she was used to living two lives.

It helped that her father was in Cape Town, a reactionary place for a reactionary job, she thought, although for many years now she had kept her true beliefs hidden from him. He was convinced that like most young people she had gone through a leftish, militant phase, and grown out of it with adulthood.

It also helped that she had been provided with the perfect cover job for her activities: an assistant to a Dutch art historian, a sympathiser. It was a job in which she had to travel a great deal.

Karen folded the letter – two pages of fiction – and sealed it ready for collection by Rolf. She stood, filled a kettle at the sink, and put it on to boil. It was a strangely domestic scene.

The house was quiet despite the number of occupants. The five prisoners were all in the cellars, confined to crudely made but effective cubicles that had been erected in preparation.

The two other guards were down there too. She had not known them before arriving, and their subservience pleased her. They would not have been told much about her; she doubted even that they had connected her with being in on the actual hijacking. But Rolf had obviously impressed them as to her importance.

She made instant coffee and stared at the envelope. Not for the first time, she fantasised his reactions if he ever found out. She'd no doubt the shock would be total. She had covered herself well. He was in his last posting now – counsellor at the Dutch Embassy in South Africa. His heart was not good, according to her mother's letters. The revelation would probably kill him. That thought amused her too.

In a funny way his job had been responsible. It was on a visit to Canada during his posting there that the first real seeds had been sown. She was on holiday from university and on the invitation of a friend's family had detoured to Quebec. The Quebec Liberation Front, which in 1970 had kidnapped a Quebec minister and a British diplomat, killing the first, was already finished as a body. But she met sympathisers who convinced her about 'liberation' and about 'freedom from colonialism' – and back in Holland she began reading Debray and Guevara, Marcuse and Marighella. She was especially drawn to Fanon and the mystique he drew for violence – an act he saw as improving in itself, a cleansing force.

By the late 1970s she was deeply involved in the Dutch 'Red Aid' organisation which had close collaboration with, especially, German, Japanese and Palestinian terrorist groups.

But her special worth as a diplomat's daughter had been noted early, and her role was an underground one: furnishing reports on Embassies, other diplomats, aircraft and airports. The Concorde hijacking had been the first *real* action, and despite the dangers (perhaps even because of them) she had welcomed it wholeheartedly. Other assignments she had carried out might have been important, but they were not what she wanted – to be out there, a soldier in the front line, succeeding gloriously or dying.

She had been chosen this time because of the importance of the job, and because, like most women terrorists, she was more fanatical, more ruthless, less given to humane thoughts than the men: it had not been coincidence that twelve of the original twenty-two members of the German Baader-Meinhof gang were women.

Still carrying her coffee cup, Karen left the kitchen and opened the heavy door leading to the basement steps.

She had a special duty today, to be carried out before Rolf's arrival, and she had been saving it. The two guards, seated at a large, oak table, nodded as she entered. The cellar was huge: four interconnecting rooms, three of which provided the cells for the five prisoners.

Between each cell there was an area of open space, so that they could not hear each other or communicate.

The doors were all closed and locked, but there were peepholes. She started with the Frenchman, he was kneeling on the floor, back to her, forehead pressed down into the mattress. He was praying. He seemed always to be praying.

She watched for several seconds, experiencing an almost sexual surge of power. But not him, she thought. Not him.

Andrew Muntwick Junior was naked but for a pair of underpants, and he had lifted the bed and turned it on to its side to give him room to lie on the stone floor. He was doing sit-ups, and despite his comfortable life regular and violent exercise had developed ridges of muscle across his abdomen. He heard the peephole shutter open and without pausing in his exercise he turned his head and winked. Rich bastard. So protected, he didn't even realise the plight he was in. Daddy's money was going to arrive and save him as it always had before, just like the cavalry in a movie.

Maybe him.

Volkov was sitting on his bed, knees up, back against the wall, a ludicrous sight. It was hard to make out what he had spread out on the bed in front of him. They were small squares of cloth, torn from his clothes, each personalised in the way it was ripped, to form representations of chess pieces. The board existed only in Volkov's mind. He heard the shutter open but did not move. Either it was something he could do something about or it wasn't. He had seen jail before. He was a survivor.

Ross was staring upwards, scratching his face even though his nails had already inflamed the skin. Karen slammed the shutter open hard so that he would know she was there, but he didn't turn.

She could still not make out the memory he raised within her. God, he was such an ugly little man. He looked a loser, a repulsive, nasty little loser. He was dressed, but she imagined the skin and the flesh under the clothes – white, flabby, clammy. It had to be.

Him. Maybe him.

The last cell was that of Jennifer North. She was asleep, and snoring. The single, rough blanket was pulled up high against her throat, but one arm lay out of the side of the bed, fingers brushing the ground.

Karen's eyes followed the arm down from the shoulder. She stared. And then she knew.

# 14

The receptionist kept Singleton waiting for over two hours.

Cappello, he was certain, was in his office, would have read his note, but was, perhaps, awaiting instructions.

Although he had slept well in London after seeing Kemp the previous day and had dozed on the flight to Milan, he was still tired and he lay back in the chair, eyes closed, the unread *Rome Daily American* on his knee.

The window was open and but for the noise from the Via Manzoni below he thought he would have drifted into sleep.

He forced himself to open his eyes. The room in which he sat was cheaply furnished: two well-used armchairs, one of which he occupied, a table covered with curling magazines, and an ancient steel desk behind which a middle-aged woman typed non-stop except when the telephone rang.

It sounded now. She listened and still holding the receiver nodded towards Singleton. "You can go in now." She gestured in the direction of one of two doors.

Behind it, Cappello sat behind another aged desk. The room was tiny and every inch of desk and shelf space was covered with books and files. Cappello himself was probably in his mid-thirties, and looked ill. His skin was yellow and his eyes flecked with red. Among the debris of papers on the desk was a plate of long-forgotten sandwiches which was being used as an ashtray.

As Singleton entered he lifted a sheet of paper and looked down at it. It was the note Singleton had sent in. It said simply, "I represent Andrew Muntwick. I would like to speak to you."

Cappello handed it back to Singleton and said in English, "I can be of service to you?"

"I am seeking someone to represent me in a property transaction," he replied, handing Cappello a second sheet of paper as he spoke.

The attorney looked down at it. It said, "I have a proposition. Can we talk? I take it this room is bugged."

"You have waited in vain, I am afraid," said Cappello. "I do not handle such things. I can give you the name of someone who does if you wish."

He took a sheet of paper and wrote. Singleton took it, thanked him and left.

He studied it as he made his way down the stairs. He would destroy it later. It said, "Mausoleum Giau Giacomo de' Medici, Cathedral, forty minutes."

Singleton was there on time. The mausoleum, inspired by Michelangelo and a major attraction, was easy to find. It was impressive, but he found himself drawn to an adjoining statue to its left – the strange and disquieting effigy of St Bartholomew, who was martyred by being flayed alive, carrying his own skin.

The American was still staring at it when Cappello arrived. The lawyer drew him away immediately; Singleton was surprised the other made no comment.

Cappello led him back out on to the coloured tile pavement of the great square, the Piazza del Duomo.

"No one followed you?" asked Cappello. He stared at Singleton. "No," he said, answering his own question, "you look like a man who knows when he is being followed."

They walked in silence for perhaps twenty minutes, then Cappello saw a cab, darted through the traffic, opened the door and rushed Singleton inside.

They left it ten minutes later. "It is best to be sure," said Capello. He led Singleton into a bar and they sat in a darkened corner. "I hope this is not some attempt at a trap," said Cappello. "I grow tired of such things. Simply because I sometimes represent people they do not like, the authorities seem to believe that I should not practise my profession."

It was, Singleton supposed, an accurate enough way of putting it – as far as it went. The reason the authorities did not like Cappello's clients was that they had often blown up or shot a score of people.

Singleton remained silent, however, waiting until the waiter had brought drinks. The walls of the booth shielded them from the few other customers. The table was lit by a flickering candle in a Chianti bottle.

Singleton reached into his breast pocket and held out a banknote. Cappello's hands retreated from the table, and his eyes swivelled. Singleton guessed what the other was thinking – an attempt was being made to plant a stolen note on him, or he was being watched and would be accused of extorting money or taking a bribe.

"It's all right," said Singleton soothingly. "I'm alone. I thought you'd find it an interesting note. I doubt you've ever seen one like it before, I'm told there are rare banknote dealers who have never set eyes on one."

He laid it on the table where Cappello could see it. It was of normal dollar bill size, black letters on a white background, the head of a man in the centre. But he knew it was the figures – printed at the top and bottom left and right hand corners and repeated in words across the bottom – that would hold Cappello's gaze.

"It's the highest value note in circulation," said Singleton. "Ten thousand dollars. Issued by the Federal Reserve Bank. As far as I know they'd still honour it, but you'd be a fool to let them have it. They stopped printing them in 1944. There are only three to four hundred left. Its real value is considerably more."

Cappello was genuinely puzzled. "Why do you tell me?"

Singleton retrieved the note. "My client collects such objects," he smiled. "I thought it might be a good way of proving how serious I am."

He lifted the note, pointed to the head in the centre – "Salmon Portland Chase, originator of the American national banking system," he said.

He turned the note and Cappello could see the reverse side, green, with an etching of what was obviously the Pilgrim Fathers embarking.

Without moving his eyes from the lawyer's face or changing his expression Singleton moved the note and placed it in the candle flame. It burst into fire almost immediately.

Cappello began to lift his hand and then stopped himself.

Singleton held the note until the flame reached his fingers and then dropped it into the ashtray. Cappello watched until there was nothing left but a blackened heap.

"What do you want of me?" he asked finally.

"I want you to pass on a message, that's all."

"To whom?"

"To someone who has got what Mr Muntwick wants. I don't think I need to be more specific."

"I know no such people."

"No, perhaps not. But I thought if I could talk with Professor Baccarri."

"He knows no such people either."

"No, but he has many friends. *If* he knew what I am offering and *if* he mentioned it to enough friends, it might reach someone who did know. Someone unknown to Professor Baccarri, of course."

Cappello leaned across the table and his voice was a whisper. "And your offer really would be a serious one?"

Singleton reached back into his breast pocket and removed a second $10,000 bill. He held it out towards the candle.

Cappello pushed it back. "I hate waste," he said. "I do not know. But tell me where you are staying. I will think."

At first Gozori had feared he was being recalled to Moscow in disgrace.

There had been no explanation. 'Return,' the message had said. And within the hour he had been collected, driven concealed in the back of a van to the outskirts of the airfield, and hurriedly placed aboard a Soviet plane that had earlier delivered a Russian delegation.

The new orders were welcome – even though they put him very much into the front line. He was to go to Paris – an Aeroflot plane was waiting as he was being briefed – and deal with the Frenchman himself.

Because the alternative reason for recall could have meant a labour camp or him 'disappearing', his relief remained an hour later when thirty thousand feet above Poland he realised why they had double checked that all his documentation was Algerian.

If anything happened to him no one must know he was a Soviet agent. His masters hoped he would succeed. But they had decided that he was expendable.

They came for Singleton at three ten in the morning. He heard the lock being forced and would have had time to react if he had wished. But he remained seated in the easy chair, fully clothed, where he had dozed half the night.

There were two, both young, both armed. They searched him, led him out and along the corridor and down a fire escape – no doubt the way they had entered.

The driver was already in the car, a black Mercedes. Singleton was placed in the back seat, between his two guards. As the car drove off, one slipped a hood over his head, and pushed him down on to the floor. Singleton did not resist.

They drove for what Singleton estimated to be about an hour before the car stopped and he was dragged, still hooded, out of the vehicle, up a staircase, along a passageway and through a door.

He blinked as the hood was removed and he concentrated on standing; his legs ached where he had been forced to lie curled.

Gradually, he took in the scene. The room was long and elegantly furnished with modern pieces. One wall was totally covered with white bookshelves. The carpet too was white, as was the sofa on which lay an ascetic-looking man with long hair which was also white.

The man, whom Singleton recognised as Baccarri, waved towards a chair. "Sit if you wish."

Singleton hobbled painfully to the chair and sat, trying not to let his face betray any sign of pain or discomfort.

Baccarri leaned forward, opened a box and extracted a cigarette which he placed in a long holder. Like almost everything else, Singleton noted, it was white.

Baccarri lit the cigarette with a large silver table lighter. "Signor Cappello tells me you would like me to deliver a message for you," he said. "I'm not sure that I'm flattered to be regarded as a messenger boy even if I were capable of delivering the kind of message you seem to have in mind."

Singleton said nothing; Baccarri would not have seen him if he were not already part-hooked. Either he had a line to the hijackers already, or he would open one. For him it would be easy. Was not he the foremost current philosopher of the terrorists, justifying their crimes, flattering their egos? Singleton remembered one of his essays: "How dare they who napalm villages full of innocent people criticise those who practice the most humane, the most selective, form of warfare. You are to be praised for your humanitarianism."

Once Baccarri had been a Professor at Padua University, long a centre of the extreme left. He had been arrested many times on suspicion of direct involvement with terrorism, but released each time for lack of evidence. Now he concentrated on his writing. His life style, Singleton decided looking around the room, hinted that his terrorist friends did not fail to show their monetary appreciation.

Baccarri waved his cigarette holder at a guard who remained in the doorway. "You must not think this is the way I like to receive my guests. It is my burden in life to have to be apprehensive of strangers – the fascists have tried to kill me many times."

He flicked ash with measured theatricality. "It is nearing dawn, Mr Singleton," he said. "Almost my bedtime. I will hear your message, but I can offer nothing."

"You know whom I represent," said Singleton. "He offers twice the amount that has been asked."

"*Money!*" Baccarri shook his head vigorously. "Will capitalists never learn?"

Singleton bit back the reply that it was the hijackers who had asked for money.

Baccarri stood, still shaking his head. He wore tight white trousers, white leather pumps, a white silk shirt wide open at the chest displaying a medallion.

"No, no, Mr Singleton. Even if I had a way of passing on a message I would not pass that."

Singleton stared into the professor's eyes. "And," he said, "we offer the seven in jail in Spain."

Baccarri looked down. "How can you do that?"

"That would be our problem. But they would be free before we would expect anything in return."

"You would want all the hostages, or just the Muntwick boy."

"For what we are offering, all of them."

Baccarri smiled. "Your friends show a trusting nature."

"I have always found that even in an enterprise like this some mutual trust is necessary."

Baccarri stubbed out his cigarette. "Is is my bedtime."

Singleton rose, but waited. There had to be more.

"I can guarantee nothing," said Baccarri. "But if I could, how should I make contact?"

Singleton took out a slip of paper. "There are five telephone numbers there," he said. "One in each of five capital cities. Each is manned twenty-four hours a day. I can be reached through any of them."

Baccarri reached out and took the paper without looking at it.

"As I said, I can guarantee nothing."

Singleton gazed into his eyes, and knew he had made contact.

# 15

They met at nine a.m. on Saturday, 13 April, inside the American Cemetery at Suresnes just outside Paris.

Singleton, who had ridden out from the Paris Hilton where he had spent the night after arriving on the Trans-Europe Express from Milan, arrived first.

He stood, staring at the memorial to a Sherman Adam Ford who had died at the age of just nineteen. Paris today was not the city of the April song. There was a blustery wind and a damp chill, and Singleton stood hunched, his collar turned high.

Kemp and Farrell found him without trouble: the Cemetery, the resting place of American soldiers killed in World War I, was almost deserted. Kemp had flown in on an early flight from London; Farrell had driven up from the south.

Neither had topcoats, and they were glad when Singleton began to walk, talking as they traversed the lines of graves. "I've made contact," said Singleton. "I'm pretty sure of that. No indication whether they'll go along with it yet, but we'll have to proceed on the assumption they will."

Farrell had most to report. "The truck's fixed," he said. "Coming over from England with a genuine load, genuine papers Monday night." He turned towards Kemp without slowing his stride. "You pick it up on this side. The driver's been bribed to stop – thinks he's going to pick up a package, doesn't know what will really happen. But we can hold him at the garage until it's over. His load's destined for Portugal – we'll be through before anyone reports him missing."

Singleton nodded appreciation. "Sounds good," he said. "And the helicopter?"

"I've found one. I can get it when the time comes." He volunteered no further information and Singleton did not ask him.

"Okay," said Singleton briskly, "let's start synchronising places and times."

It was thirty-five minutes before each of them was satisfied.

They left separately, Singleton first. "The number will reach me if you need me," he said.

"Where'll you be?" asked Kemp.

"On a shopping trip, and briefing our rich master."

The cab was still waiting at the entrance when Singleton emerged.

"You find the one you wanted?" asked the driver sympathetically.

"I found it."

The brown paper-covered parcel was delivered in the post just about the time Singleton's cab was nearing the airport for his flight to Chicago.

It was addressed to the legal attaché at the American Embassy in London. Like all parcels it was scanned first for explosives. Then because 'legal attaché' is a euphemism for the ranking FBI man at an embassy it was submitted to further checks.

Because of these, it was a full half-hour before the final layer of paper was removed and the lid was carefully raised from the small plastic box that was revealed.

Inside there was cotton wool, and a security guard lifted it carefully with a pair of long tweezers. The FBI man, who had been called in from home, watched carefully. Something fell out, a long thin piece of wrinkled plastic.

Only it wasn't. It was a woman's finger and on it there was a ring. There was no message, but there was no need for one. Anyone who read gossip columns knew about the ring with its huge sapphire, her birthstone.

The FBI man knew immediately what it was. Jennifer North's finger.

There was a car waiting for Singleton when he arrived at O'Hare airport, and soon after six he was back in Muntwick's office.

Singleton was conscious immediately of a change of atmosphere since he and Muntwick had first talked six days before. Then, because Singleton had brought hope, it had been close, almost friendly. Now it was formal. Singleton was an employee doing a job, important though it might be.

Singleton summarised his progress. Muntwick's lack of responses made him stress how much he had done, the visits to half a dozen different places in three countries. But Muntwick seemed unimpressed – a man who took such things as a matter of course.

"There are only seven days until their deadline," said Muntwick finally, as though he had heard nothing. "You still think you can do it?"

"I think so."

Muntwick stood and walked around the desk, and Singleton noted that although the man wore a formal suit his feet were clad in old carpet slippers.

"So what do you want from me? Why do you waste time reporting to me in person? I've got offices with secure communications in Europe."

"I need three things."

"Name them."

"First, I need the use of the spa you own." They had discussed this during Singleton's first visit.

"It's yours. Do you want me to move people out?"

"No. It would just attract attention."

"And?" Impatiently.

"I'll need the use of one of your tankers." Singleton put down his cup, fumbled in his pockets and produced a sheet of paper. "These are details of time and location."

Muntwick barely glanced at it. "A small problem. Done."

"And one last thing," Singleton continued. He produced a

second piece of paper from his pocket. On it were figures and measurements given to him by Kemp.

"I hope you've still got companies that produce anti-riot equipment," he said, handing it to Muntwick.

Muntwick took the paper. "I do," he said. "Got in early. Still one of the fastest growing businesses in the West." He studied the details carefully. "Looks a simple enough technical problem," he said.

"I'll need a dozen of them, and fast."

"When do you leave?"

"Tomorrow night from Washington. I still have things to finalise there."

Muntwick pressed a button on his desk and said into the air, "Get me Dawson at Northland Systems. I want him now. Track him down wherever he is."

"You'll have them," he said to Singleton.

The apartment was in the ritzy sixteenth district, a studio room with a kitchenette and a small bathroom just large enough to hold a hip bath.

It was on the third floor and there was no lift and Gozori was breathing heavily as the concierge led him inside.

"I *knew* there was something wrong with him," she said with a small note of triumph in her voice. "Always away, coming and going at all hours." She was in her late fifties, dressed in black and had been eating alone when Gozori had arrived. He noted the bitterness in her voice, and told himself he knew her kind. Such women made good informers all over the world. Ideal for his purpose, though.

There had been no problem from the moment Gozori had shown her his forged Sûreté credentials. He had decided earlier that the direct approach was best; why break in when you could be let in by key?

"You will tell no one, please, Madam," he said, looking around the room. "Remember what I said: a life may be at stake."

He had no doubt that she would talk, but not yet, not while

he was around, not while her tenant was still expected to return soon.

The woman had already told Gozori that Gabriel Hardy had come back to the apartment three days before after a week's absence. He had gone out that morning. She thought he would return that day, he had taken no case. "But he may be late, Monsieur Inspecteur – it is Saturday and he is young."

Gozori watched her go, closed the door, slid off his coat and began to search the room. He found two spare passports taped to the underside of a bureau drawer, an address book which he pocketed, and a large collection of maps of European cities under the carpet. There were also three pistols, wrapped in three layers of waterproof material, and suspended in the lavatory tank.

Finally satisfied, Gozori broke the seal on an unopened bottle of armagnac he found in the kitchenette, carried it into the main room and lay down on the sofa, facing the door. He was impatient, but he knew there was nothing to do but wait.

It was almost eleven and Singleton lay on the bed in his hotel room watching television, exhausted but oddly awake.

He was still fully clothed although he knew he should sleep; he had already contacted Warren and had arranged a meeting for the next morning.

He was tensed anyway, but the newscast he had just watched did not help. He kept thinking about Debbie, and how she would have been eleven now. Almost drunkenly – although he was far from drunk – he leaned over and pushed his whisky glass away so that it skidded on the glass top of the bedside table, spilling a trail of liquid.

He stared at the ceiling and found he was crying, something he could not remember doing since the night he'd heard she was dead. God, he felt himself muttering, everyone knew measles didn't kill anyone. Except it had.

Singleton pulled himself up, switched off the television, stripped, showered, re-dressed and picked up the telephone.

She was a long time answering and he had begun to fear her apartment was empty.

"I'm in Washington," he said. "Can I come and see you?"

"You presume a lot," she said. "I was in bed. How do you know I'm alone?"

"I don't."

"You'd better give me half an hour."

What did that mean? That there was a man with her? That, simply, she wanted time to make up, to prepare?

For a moment he wished he had not called. Then he knew it had been inevitable. He had to go.

She opened the door as soon as he rang. She was wearing the towelling robe he had worn less than a week before.

She wore no make-up and, inside, the living room was untidied. There was a whiff of pipe tobacco and the room was cold as though the window had been opened wide. It had been a man. Strange, he had never thought of lovers until this night; perhaps it was too obvious and, in any event, something he did not wish to dwell upon.

As he accepted a drink, he asked himself how he felt. Surprisingly, he felt good about it. It was good for her that there were others; it was a tribute to the special relationship between the two of them that she dismissed one to welcome him. He found himself suddenly amused and intrigued, wondering how she had dealt with the man, how she had persuaded him to leave and whether it would have looked like a French farce as the man had gathered his clothes.

"Is it a bad one?" she asked, handing him the glass.

He didn't answer, but he reached out and drew her against him. She smelled of soap and talcum powder. She had bathed. So she and the man had made love. There were times when it would have angered him, others when the sexuality of it would have stirred him more than usual. Tonight it seemed to matter little.

"Let's go to bed," he said.

Afterwards, even though love-making had lasted longer than usual for them, neither could sleep. She was the first to speak. "You're going away again straight away?"

He did not answer; he raised what had been on his mind for hours. "Did you watch the newscasts on television tonight?" he asked.

"No." Puzzled. "Should I have?"

Her reply did not matter. He had to talk.

"There was a scene shot at the airport in Geneva. A camera crew was passing through on some assignment, so they filmed it soon after it happened."

"The bomb attack? I heard it on the radio."

He continued as though he had not heard her. "There was a kid, a girl, six, seven, I guess. I don't know. I had the sound off and didn't dare to turn it up. She was lying among the wreckage, one leg blown off, while doctors tried to keep her alive and rescue workers tried to free her."

"I know. I heard. She died."

"Did she? I guessed she would."

Singleton stared up in the blackness. He could see the child's face, strangely composed, full of trust.

"I kept thinking it could have been Debbie," he said at last.

"Was what you saw anything to do with what you're doing?" Kate asked quietly.

At first she thought he was not going to reply. Then he turned, wrapped an arm around her, and began to talk. "So these are the kind of people I'll free. But I *have* to."

For the first time ever, he not only told her, but he told her everything. She did not know what to reply at first and then it was too late. She heard his breathing, deep, rhythmic. He was asleep. It was as though talking had given him absolution and peace.

It was just before four a.m. when Gozori heard the key turn in the lock.

The bottle of armagnac beside him was three-quarters empty but he was sober and wide awake. He swung himself off the bed without a sound and stood silent in the darkness.

He waited until the man was inside the room and had turned to close the door before he moved. He raised his right leg and kicked Hardy with all his strength in the middle of his back.

The man shot forward, his face crashing into the door full-on. There was surprisingly little noise.

Gozori moved back and clicked on the light. Hardy, crumbled on to his knees, heaved himself and turned. Blood gushed from his nose; a split over his right eye gaped open. Despite his injuries, his hand was clawing instinctively for his gun.

"Easy!"

He paused at Gozori's command. His eyes focussed on the Russian's hand. In it there was a pistol. "Yours," said Gozori conversationally. "You recognise it?"

Hardy stared at the weapon – an Astra .357 magnum. A real assassination weapon, a gun with such power that at this range it could not fail to kill.

"Who are you?" He tried to pull himself to his feet.

Gozori's foot caught him in the side of his mouth, smashing his head back into the door again. He slid down, only half conscious.

Gozori moved backwards, sat on the edge of the bed, reached for his glass of armagnac. His eyes stared at Hardy's body. Although he was in a hurry, he would wait. It was vital that the Frenchman was in the right frame of mind.

Even though the National Museum of Natural History had only been open ten minutes it was already filled with April Washington visitors.

Most, though, were still grouped near the entrance, gazing up at the largest African elephant shot in our time, or studying the spectacularly mounted exhibits around.

Singleton passed through them, and made straight for the African weapons and musical instruments section. Warren was already there, standing alone by the glass-fronted mud and bamboo Bantu hut.

At Singleton's approach he walked away, through a door marked Private, down a deserted corridor and into an unmarked room. Singleton followed, and Warren turned the key behind them.

The room was small and empty but for a bucket and a polishing machine.

Both men carried copies of the *New York Times* Sunday edition, and they exchanged them without preliminaries.

"The latest shots," said Warren. The US had modified the orbit of a Big Bird Supersatellite to pass over the Spanish prison where the terrorists were held. Its Perkins Elmer very high resolution camera had picked up objects of even a foot in length from a hundred miles up. The film, in cannisters, had been ejected into the earth's atmosphere and picked up over the Pacific the previous day.

Singleton nodded, but did not bother to open the paper – he would do that later. "There're also drawings from American firms that took part in the construction, and an Embassy report – the Spaniards invited some parties along once it was finished to show them how secure and humane it all was."

"Good."

The room was lit by one neon tube in the ceiling, and Warren moved forward and peered into Singleton's face. "You look tired," he volunteered. "It's still all right?" he continued. "You still think you can make it?"

"I've been travelling and, yes, I'm tired. And, yes, I think we can make it."

Warren checked his watch. "Is there any more you need from me?"

"Just two things. Most I can arrange myself."

"Okay. Shoot."

"The first is a package. I'll have it later today. It's pretty small, about the size of one volume of an encyclopaedia. But it's delicate, and I need it in France or Spain."

"And you want it delivered?"

"Yes. I can't take the chance trying to get it through."

"Okay. That's easy. It'll just be something else secret in the pipeline. But I'd prefer France. It keeps it more distant. Okay?"

"As long as it gets there fast."

"It will." He listed instructions for the handover and later collection.

"I've got it."

"There was one more?"

Singleton rubbed his eyes, moved to the corner of the small room, upturned the empty bucket and used it as a seat.

He did not answer the question immediately, despite the CIA chief's obvious desire to get away quickly.

"Did you see the late night news last night?" he asked. "There were some shots of a bombing in Geneva. Did you see it?" He had made his decision on the way from Kate's.

"Yes, I guess I did." Warren's voice was puzzled.

"Did you see the kid, the one whose leg got blown off. Did you see it?"

"Yeah. You don't often get a camera crew on the spot like that." His embarrassment with the intensity in Singleton's voice made him keep his own tone even more emotionless than usual.

"Tape worms," Singleton said quietly. "What happened to them, Cord?"

Warren's face became shocked. "You shouldn't even know the name," he said.

'Tape worm' was a pill, a CIA chemist's contribution to the dirty-tricks department in 1980. They had never been tried as far as Singleton knew, but he was familiar with the theory: a capsule covered with gelatin which rapidly dissolved in the body, revealing a second capsule covered with dozens of miniscule hooks.

These were intended to anchor themselves to the walls of the intestine. The coating of the inner capsule – a specially formulated protein – would take upwards of a week to be eaten away by the enzymes. Then a poison inside would bring instant death. By that time the assassin could be far away. There had been talk at one time of using them to kill the Ayatollah Khomeini in a way that would absolve the Americans of any suspicion.

"I was around Iran at the time. There was talk of them . . ."

"No one ever took them seriously. One of those mad things. Give a scientist enough dollars and facilities and . . . well, you know."

"What happened to them?"

"As soon as anyone knew what was going on, they were destroyed. Every damn one of them."

Singleton looked up, his eyes cold. "I want some, Cord," he said.

"I told you they were destroyed."

"No one destroys things like that. You may move them, hide them a whole lot better, stick a new lock on the safe. But you don't get rid of them."

"It's asking too much, George."

Singleton pulled himself up and clutched the newspaper under his arm.

"I'll free your prisoners, Cord," he said. "You'll have what you want. I'll die if I have to. So will the others involved." His voice was as bleak, as emotionless as Warren's had been moments before. "I don't ask for money. I don't want kudos.

"But there's a price. I've just named it. And you'd better pay it."

Kemp spent his Sunday morning amidst the noise and bustle of an East London street market.

It was midday before he had finished fighting his way through the crowds that thronged the stalls that covered the roadway for well over a mile.

By then his arms were filled with brown paper packages. The pub was hardly quieter than the street outside, but he found a corner seat, spread his parcels around his feet and sipped a pint glass of bitter beer.

As he drank he reviewed his morning's shopping, checking mentally whether he had everything.

As his eyes scanned the parcels, he made mental ticks: a navy blue, second-hand workman's donkey-jacket; a cap;

two flannel shirts; an ex-army sweater, grey with elbow patches; a pair of heavy, rubber-soled shoes . . .

Only one more thing, he concluded: a suitcase, preferably not new. He would buy that on his way to the rental company where he would pick up the van.

They made love in a bedroom rubble of half-eaten croissants, empty coffee cups, and fresh oranges that filled the room with their perfume.

Afterwards Farrell and Martine slept, their naked bodies curled together.

Farrell woke first, turned his head, and saw that the time was just after twelve twenty. He eased himself out of bed, and without showering began to dress. He was a fastidious man, but for reasons that he did not bother to focus upon he wanted to retain the feel and smell of sex. He also, more prosaically, wanted to be on his way before she woke. Although they separated often, partings grew more difficult. There was always a hurt in her eyes, no matter what words she spoke.

There was a pad on the oak dresser and he wrote the briefest of notes: "Love you. I'll hurry back. Be good. Take care." He signed it with a bad sketch of a squirrel – for some reason that had never been clear, she always called him 'My mad squirrel'.

He kissed her forehead, and she moved and lifted a hand to stroke back her hair. But she did not wake. And at twelve forty-five Farrell slid into the passenger seat beside his driver and was on his way south.

The parcel from Muntwick was delivered to Singleton at his hotel just after five thirty p.m. and handed over at the designated point for Warren less than an hour later.

There was a message at the airport, unsigned, but, Singleton knew, from Warren.

"Agreed," it said.

* * *

At the time he should have been on his way to Paris Singleton was airbound once again for Chicago.

At the last moment, after twenty minutes careful thought, he had changed his mind. At eleven p.m. he was standing in front of a puzzled and slightly angry Muntwick. Despite the day, Sunday, and the late hour, Muntwick was still at his desk, obviously still working.

"There are problems? You didn't get what you wanted?"

"No problems, and yes, I got what I wanted."

"So?"

Singleton explained.

"You ask a great deal," Muntwick said finally.

Singleton shuffled, but said nothing.

"All right," said the billionaire at last. "I confess to sharing your feelings – I imagine that's what it's all about.

"But" – and the rasp hung in the air – "don't let it get in the way of what really matters."

Farrell lay on his back on the massive iron-headboard bed in the small room overlooking the narrow Montpellier side street.

He had left his driver at Nîmes. There the man would pick up a rental car the following morning, making sure it was in order to return it to another branch in Marseilles.

Then he would drive to meet Farrell in Montpellier, where he lay now, hands clasped behind his neck, too excited to sleep.

It was good to be working with Singleton again – to his mind one of the few 'spooks' he had met who, despite his implacable features, had a heart. He remembered him in Vietnam. Singleton had helped him leave without problems: those who upped and went, as Farrell had, were quickly suspect. What happened to them could depend on just how suspect, and what friends they had.

But it was later, when Farrell was building his smuggling empire, that he remembered their co-operation most. The occasions had not been numerous, but there was one in particular.

Singleton had a meeting arranged on the Soviet side of the Turkish-USSR border. Farrell was recruited, not to fly but because he had good smuggling contacts in Turkey.

Farrell knew nothing of the meeting itself – Singleton had volunteered no more than he had to – but they had been ambushed. Farrell remembered Singleton running under fire to help him and a wounded Turkish guide, little more than a boy, who was shot and whom Farrell was trying to help.

Farrell remembered Singleton probably saving his life. The irony was that he did not know that Singleton remembered the incident not that way, but of Farrell saving the young Turk's life.

The problem he faced now, Farrell thought, was not a particularly difficult one. He estimated he had plenty of time. Tomorrow, with the help of an insider, he would pinpoint the location of the firm's helicopters.

The company that interested him supplied craft for charter work and for crop spraying. In reality, its existence was far from unconnected with the heroin factories in the countryside.

Farrell knew this, and had contacts, because as a smuggler it was his job to know such things, even though he himself had never handled narcotics.

Farrell had toyed with the idea of getting his hands on a helicopter legitimately – chartering one, even buying one. But such possibilities carried their own dangers.

It was easier to steal one. And much safer. It would be days before this particular company reported the theft – if at all.

Farrell turned, reached out and lifted the photograph of Martine that he had propped on the bedside table. He looked at it for a long time before turning out the light and drifting into an uneasy sleep filled with whirring blades.

# 16

The helicopters began swooping down over the eight-foot-high wire-mesh fences and into the 143-acre Camp David site late morning Monday, 15 April.

They carried editors of major newspapers, agencies and networks for a news conference with a difference.

As they arrived, they were escorted by blue-blazered Navy stewards into the grey-green main residence where the President was already waiting.

Although it was not quite noon a table was laden with a buffet luncheon, and another of the stewards – the presidential seal decorating his breast pocket – handed out glasses of Californian white wine.

President Proctor, himself looking tired and aged, sipped Indian tonic water: with the medication he now took to help him sleep, to lower his blood pressure, and to give him energy, he did not dare risk alcohol.

The President circulated, engaging in small talk until every visitor was present. Then he wasted no time in explaining why the conference was different: he planned to brief them on everything that was happening, but he was asking that not a word be printed.

There were immediate mutterings and groans: Proctor had been under media attack for several days for failing to take the country into his confidence.

Most publishers and news executives accepted that there were limits to what might be said. But the President appeared to be pursuing a policy of secrecy for its own sake.

There was not even confirmation or denial of a widely

reported story that the hijackers had cut off and sent one of Jennifer North's fingers.

Nevertheless the newsmen now confined their murmurings to themselves, awed as always by the presidential presence – the post, not the man – and curious about the various advisers present, who included members of the co-ordinating committee.

Proctor introduced them, paused, then said, with a forced laugh, spreading his hands, "You've nothing you want to say to me?"

There was laughter from the editors too before one voice was raised. "Mr President," began Johnson of the *Washington Post*, "I think I speak not only for those of us here but also for a majority of people in the country when I say the nation needs to be taken more into your confidence."

Proctor raised a hand to still the murmurs of agreement and to head off more comments. "Let me fill you in," he said.

He talked for forty minutes, detailing everything that was known, all that had been done, all that would be done. Then he began to defend his secrecy policy.

"What it comes down to, gentlemen, is not anything startling. It is that neither we nor the Soviet Union is going to give way. We stand totally firm." He pointed dramatically to a grandfather clock at the far end of the room. "We still hope that we can find the hostages before the deadline expires. We don't *want* them to die. We are doing everything that is possible, as I have told you."

His voice became conspiratorial. "We are also trying to pass to them a message that will persuade them to extend their deadline, giving us more time."

It changed to being statesmanlike. "It is in our interests to let them *think* we might still negotiate. Once they receive confirmation that we won't budge an inch, then . . ." He chopped downwards with one hand dramatically.

"But it's more than that. Anything we do – anything at all – that appears to encourage the hijackers in a course of action will be seen as a calculated, unfriendly action by the Soviets. I need hardly tell you that's the last thing we want at this time. President Bukashev has gone a long way to restoring a genuine détente after the last desperate days of Brezhnev and his immediate successor."

Long before Proctor had finished it was obvious that he had won over most of his audience, enemies as well as supporters. They would go along, albeit reluctantly, with the policy of a news blackout.

The official part of the gathering ended, stewards re-entered, filled glasses, distributed food.

Proctor resumed circulating. He did not know Craven of the *St Petersburgh Times* by sight, but Watson did and the aide nudged him and whispered, "That's him."

Proctor caught the man's eye and nodded. He wanted to be affable but not get caught in a situation where he had to talk to the man now.

Craven's paper had carried a report the previous Friday bylined by a reporter called Ralph Leger. In a routine way it had been read with all other reports about the search for the terrorists. One paragraph, buried two thirds of the way through the article, had attracted the notice of one of the researchers, even though he did not think it important, and he had marked it and passed it on.

Bill Watson had not seen it until that, Monday, morning when he had stumbled upon it. The marked paragraph raised the possibility that the organisation Ross worked for was a front for an American government agency. It was explained no further, but Watson had talked to the President.

It was a line of investigation that had to be shut off quickly.

One aid with which the KGB did not supply their agents was any form of credit card – unless they were operating in a country as natives under 'deep cover'.

Which was why reception scrutinised Gozori very carefully in Paris that same morning as he checked into a hotel, desperate to enjoy his first real sleep for three days.

At a lesser hotel than the *George V* the receptionist would have probably asked for money in advance. But that would have been unthinkable here. He would content himself by asking security to keep a special watch.

If he noticed any hesitation Gozori showed no sign. Apart from the need to sleep, his mind was too preoccupied with what he had done: turned Hardy free to carry the message that the Russians were prepared to 'buy' their minister in a separate deal.

His actions had been ordered. He had done no more than he had been told.

But, as he watched the bell-boy leave, tossed off his coat, and flopped fully dressed on to the bed, that did not help his worries.

If things went wrong there was no doubt who would take the blame.

Singleton was in the same city, equally tired, enjoying equal luxury without the time or mood to appreciate it.

His room had been booked at the *Crillon*, nicely convenient for the American Embassy. Which probably helped explain the smoothness of the handover.

The bell rang an hour after he had checked in. He had eaten in his room and the tray still lay waiting for collection. He was on his second cup of coffee.

When he opened the door the bell-boy clutched a Samsonite briefcase bearing a luggage tab and Singleton's name.

"You left a case downstairs," said the boy.

Singleton tipped him, carried the case inside, checked that it was locked, drew a selection of picks from his pocket, and heard both locks click open in less than five minutes.

Kemp's 'order' was packed in layers of cotton wool surrounded by polystyrene. They took up less than half the case. There was also an unmarked screw top metal container, about three inches long and an inch in diameter. Singleton unscrewed the top and shook out one of the capsules – small, torpedo shaped, red and green, reminiscent of cold relief tablets.

There was also a name and a telephone number – the one he had wanted in Bilbao.

Finally, there was a small, flat box, which he opened carefully.

In it there was a silver dollar. He removed it and stared at it without expression.

He knew what it was, knew that if he twisted it, the face side would spring open revealing a quarter-inch needle on a spring. Under a microscope the needle would be seen to be grooved like a drill-bit.

It was one of the agency's better inventions, the successor to the wartime cyanide L-pill which OSS agents had carried. That pill had killed all right, but only after anything up to fifteen agonising minutes.

This needle's grooves were impregnated with shellfish toxin. One prick, almost instantaneous tingling in the fingers and lips showing it was working – and death, painlessly from paralysis, within ten seconds.

Singleton had not asked for it, and there was no note. But Warren's message could not have been clearer.

By mid-evening of the same day Farrell, over two hundred miles south of Paris, had narrowed down his search to two specific helicopters.

One was parked just outside the hangar of the small airstrip of the company he had decided upon; the other, also owned by them, was being used for crop-spraying twenty miles away. The job looked like a long one, and the craft was left in the fields, locked and covered with a tarpaulin.

Theoretically, both were too small for the assignment – lifting seven men, plus, of course, himself in the pilot's seat.

The helicopter outside the hangar was a Bell Jetranger 206B. The one out crop-spraying was also American, an Enstrom 280L Hawk.

The Bell was designed to carry five, the Enstrom four. Farrell wanted a small helicopter, though, because of the space restrictions for his landing at the prison. The small exercise yard Singleton wanted him to use was little more than fifty feet wide, allowing not much more than a man's height clearance each side of the rotor blades. Tight, much tighter than many helicopter pilots would consider safely possible even in ideal conditions. And Farrell planned to come in fast in the dark.

Back in his hotel room, he sat in the single chair, the unheard radio babble of noise in the background, and deliberated.

The Bell had two advantages. It was faster – a top speed of 145 mph instead of 117 – but that fact was marginal. More useful was the fact that it had only two rotor blades. They could be turned to run parallel with the craft itself and the helicopter could thus be loaded into the trailer that Kemp was to drive through France just as it was.

The Enstrom, on the other hand, had three rotor blades, so they would have to be removed before the craft could be winched into the trailer and then replaced later. Not a hard job, but it took some time. Replacement time, though, could be cut to a minimum. Theoretically, they should be replaced using a torque spanner to ensure just the right amount of tension. For his purposes, however, Farrell thought he could just screw the 'Jesus nut' tight – it wouldn't last long, but then it wasn't meant to.

And the lifting problem? Again the Bell had the edge. It was designed to lift about 1700 pounds compared with 1100 pounds for the Enstrom. But again that was not crucial in practice. He could strip the chosen helicopter of everything that was not necessary – radio, many of the instruments, even the upholstery off the seats – and he could carry no more fuel than was necessary. For the rest, he could depend on the high safety margin the manufacturers built in when they specified so-called 'maximum' weights to be carried.

He was still deliberating when the call came: Singleton had left the bag in a left luggage locker at Toulouse airport and would now move on to Spain.

Farrell suddenly became conscious of the radio, clicked it off, poured a brandy and decided.

The Enstrom. There was little in the size – it had thirty-four foot rotor blades, the Bell thirty-three foot four inches, not enough difference to matter. But – the key thing – it was easier to steal – and he should have longer before its loss was discovered.

He poured a brandy and began to sweat. He hoped no one would move it before tomorrow night.

Kemp pulled the van off the slip road to Newhaven docks just as the sky was beginning to darken.

No one would bother him here; many drivers, waiting to catch the last ferry of the night at ten p.m., paused after a long journey to rest, to eat sandwiches, to drink tea from a flask.

The truck came past forty minutes later – there was no mistaking it even without checking the licence plates: 'Zedline Carriers' in brilliant red against a green background.

He noted it first in his mirror, watched it pass, and then drew out to follow it to the docks. It was seven forty-two p.m. Once at the docks they would go separate routes, Kemp into the queue to join the ferry, the truck driver first to his firm's agents to collect his documentation then to Customs, and only then to the boat.

That did not matter, though. The important part was confirmation that the truck was on schedule. Kemp was also pleased to note it was a tractor unit he had driven before – a big Volvo, hauling a forty-foot-long box trailer.

He could, he boasted, drive anything. But with this he would not even need minutes to familiarise himself. That would be important the next day. Because in roughly eighteen hours time, down in the south of France, he would take over this truck.

Kemp swung into line for the ferry, killed the engine and settled back to wait. He closed his eyes and began picturing a hawk at the stoop.

# 17

The spa was sixty miles further west from Bilbao, one of many in the province of Santander and a bare ten miles from the town of the same name.

It was on a small islet, joined to the mainland by a short stretch of narrow road.

Its clients were the old and the rich; most of them arrived by boat or by private plane on the spa's landing strip. They included Muntwick – who had bought the spa resort eight years before when a scandal involving Solares Spa water hit the fortunes of other spas in the region. Muntwick, who had been a regular attender, heard rumours of its closure, and moved in.

It was in Muntwick's small villa at the spa that Singleton woke just after eight. The room had been painted white and was bare of all ornaments and decoration – a factor that made it hard for several minutes for him to focus on his whereabouts.

He swung himself out of bed and parted the blinds: a cluster of similar small villas faced him. Few were occupied now; for most visitors the weather was still too cold.

Singleton walked through to the kitchen/diner and spooned coffee into the percolator. Someone had already called while he slept, leaving a basket of rolls.

Biting on one, as he waited for the coffee to heat, Singleton walked through the rest of the single-storey house. The living room was as stark as the bedroom. There was one other room, and that was locked, but Singleton had a key, given to him the previous night. Inside, it was much more lived in: a sofa, a small desk and chair, a collection of notepads and pencils, a clock showing time zones, a small computer and a battery of telephones.

It was from here that Muntwick kept in touch with his empire when he was taking his thrice-yearly rest-cures.

And it was from here, using the scrambled telephone, or the two-way radio concealed in a cupboard, that Singleton would keep in touch with the message centres in five countries.

From here, he would monitor and direct events until it was time for action.

Rolf, Karen and a third terrorist, Dieter Hofmann, held a meeting in the kitchen of the Liège house early afternoon.

Hofmann, who had arrived mid-morning and then slept for two hours, as though he had undertaken a long and tiring journey, led the discussions.

He began with an order brought from Germany: the prisoners were to be moved. They had already been in one place longer than was advisable.

He continued with the raising of a question: what follow-up, if any, should be made to reinforce the warning made by cutting off Jennifer North's finger.

"Tape the Muntwick boy pleading for his life," suggested Rolf. "I'd just need a half-hour with him."

"Not enough," said Karen. "It's time for a body."

"Who?"

"Who else? Ross. He's not worth anything alive. No one cares what happens to him. He adds nothing to our bargaining strength. But dead . . ."

"What would you do?"

She lit a fresh cigarette, conscious of the eyes upon her. "A few marks to make people outside worry about what the others are experiencing – you know, a few burns, a bruise, something broken. Then a shot in the head. We could leave the body in Brussels. That would be a good place."

Hofmann turned to Rolf. "What do you think?"

Rolf didn't think it mattered one way or the other. But he

did want to improve his chances of making Karen. She had been surprisingly unresponsive, frigid almost.

"We lose nothing killing him. As Karen says, it adds to the pressure."

Hofmann pushed back his chair. Alone of the three present, he knew about the approaches that had been made by the Americans and by the Russians, both anxious to make unofficial, secret deals.

He could refer back, but he had the power to make a decision is he wished.

He knew they were waiting, but he needed to think it through.

"No," he said at last. "Let him live for now. Let's leave it as it is. They know we're serious."

He caught the girl's face. Expressionless, but he knew anger was there. "Let's get them ready to leave," he said briskly. "There'll be a truck with a hidden compartment after dark."

Then to Rolf. "You stay here in Belgium. We may need you later."

And to the girl, partly to appease her, because it had not been planned. "You come with us. We may still have to do what you suggest."

The news that the hijackers were willing to go along with the deal came on Singleton's one o'clock call.

It was a terse, coded message – words as suggested by Singleton in Italy. But they would, he knew, call the contact number again within the next few hours, for that was part of the arrangement too.

He fed in the message that he wanted to make 'local contact' and sat back impatiently to wait.

Dan Halloran was forty-one and had been a trucker for fifteen years, ever since losing his job with the close down of a car-spares factory near Birmingham.

He had drifted into trucking, then found he had liked the freedom, the solitude and the chance to make money the taxman never saw. He had worked for most types of operation – the big, reputable firms that played it by the book, and the small firms, far from reputable and often dangerously close to bankruptcy, for whom you drove so many hours non-stop that you experienced hallucinations . . .

He had run furniture to the Middle East, glass jars to Spain, machinery to Turkey. And often something else too – a few things on the side.

For more than half his years as a trucker, Halloran had earned more from the illicit extras of his work than he had from the job itself. But he had always been careful; had never been arrested, had only once been suspected – and then the evidence was pitifully inadequate.

This particular load was vehicle parts for a factory near Oporto, Portugal. The job had been arranged quickly to give cover to the real purpose of the journey. The firm for which he worked was as crooked, and careful, as he was.

The real load was a 'front'; somewhere near Bordeaux he would pick up a parcel – drugs, he thought – and conceal it in the specially converted diesel tank.

Because the job had been arranged so quickly, he had had to cross on the Newhaven-Dieppe route – not one of the drivers' favourite ones but, for that reason, usually with a vacant place. Longer ferry journeys – like Southampton to Le Havre – allowed you to sleep, put you in peak condition for the run on the other side. Newhaven-Dieppe unloaded you after four hours, at two in the morning, groggy with fatigue.

Halloran ate as he drove. If he kept legal hours – by law drivers were restricted to eight hours or 281 miles – the journey to Portugal would take four and a half to five days. He would do it in three, paying fines if he were stopped.

If he drove non-stop, except for picking up the package, he would be near the Spanish border in about eighteen hours, ready to cross next morning after sleeping in the bunk behind the driving seat.

He reached Tours mid-afternoon, nicely on schedule, and joined the small stretch of motorway that led to Poitiers.

He was feeling a second wind, and he slipped a fresh cassette into the truck's stereo player.

Singleton's first meeting took place in a pavement café in Santander at five thirty p.m. It had been arranged so quickly that he suspected that the hijackers must have made contact with the ETA Basques before letting him know they accepted his proposal.

It was a brief, nervous meeting. Singleton spoke, the elderly man in the black suit and rimless glasses sipped beer and listened. Then he slid away into the direction of the Place de Generalisimo, leaving Singleton counting days and thinking about Kemp and Farrell.

Gozori was back at Hardy's apartment, and his anger was intensified by the fact that he had run out of both armagnac and cigarettes.

He spent his time playing with the guns, loading and unloading them, aiming at imaginary targets.

The deadline had expired and there was still no word. He had been ordered to turn Hardy loose after putting the proposition to him. But if Hardy failed to return Gozori had no doubts about what would happen. The little men always went first; the higher up the ladder you were, the easier it was to save yourself.

Gozori was conscious too that his nerve was close to going: he *needed* the drink and the cigarettes that he had not got. He debated leaving the apartment briefly, just long enough to shop.

He convinced himself that he would not be long, that his temporary absence would not matter. He was pulling on his coat when he heard the footsteps on the stairs. He froze and slid the Astra off the table.

There were taps at the door. "It's me – Hardy."

Gozori slipped the chain, stepped back and covered the door. "It's open."

He had only heard one set of footsteps but he imagined others outside, all with guns, all set to get him. He was conscious of his heart thumping, of his dry mouth, his sticky hands. They *should* recall him, they really should. He had been good; surely he had done enough? There was a limit to the strain any man could take.

Hardy was alone.

As he closed the door behind him Gozori let his fear emerge in his rebuke. "You're late!" he spat.

"It wasn't easy."

"And?"

"I've someone who will talk to you."

Knowing the truck's route and having a faster vehicle, Kemp was able to keep in contact with the Volvo even though he made several stops.

Nearly fifty miles north of Bordeaux, though, he made sure he was close behind it; he would stay there until they reached the scheduled meeting place about fifteen miles further on.

Beside him, on the passenger seat, he had a parcel that he had put together at one of the stops. It was a foot square, wrapped in brown paper, heavily sealed with adhesive tape. It looked interesting. Its contents were in fact a half-dozen folded newspapers.

A signpost came into view; Kemp checked the name. According to Farrell's directions the lay-by should be no more than five to ten minutes away now.

The lay-by, deep back from the road, was quiet, but the arrangements were such that a handover could have taken place unnoticed even if it were busy. Nevertheless, the quiet made Kemp's task easier.

He drew up at the side of the Volvo, opened his door and leaned out, the parcel in his arms. The truck driver, who had moved over to the passenger side of his compartment, swung his door wide and bent over to take the package.

It was ridiculously easy. He was already unbalanced when Kemp grasped his wrists and pulled. He half turned in the air before striking the ground. He was too shocked, too winded, too dazed to offer any resistance, but Kemp had the pad ready. He plunged it over the man's face, and began heaving him into the van at the side time.

A third man joined them – one of Farrell's men, left at the lay-by an hour before to wait. He grasped the truck driver's feet, then helped slide him over the seats into the back of the van.

The truck driver was unconscious now, but they bound and gagged him quickly. Neither Kemp nor Farrell's man spoke.

That completed, Kemp slid out of the van and pulled himself up into the truck. Farrell's man finished throwing the empty sacks over the truck driver's body, got into the driving seat and pulled away. He would get rid of the van and deliver the driver to a house where he would be kept a week and then turned loose. Beyond what he personally had to do he knew nothing of what was involved.

Kemp watched him go, and then checked over the instruments to re-familiarise himself. He drove to the exit of the lay-by and waited until there was a clear road as far as he could see before pulling out; although he knew the truck it would take him a few minutes to get used to the gears.

At Bordeaux Halloran would have continued south towards the border, but Kemp detoured south-east towards Toulouse.

He drove carefully. He did not want to be stopped, even though he had already substituted his own forged passport and driving licence for Halloran's among the documents.

Any traffic policeman who examined the papers, though, would see that Kemp had diverted from his route. He had a story if that happened: a girl in Toulouse – but he would rather not have to risk it.

He reached the garage on the outskirts of Toulouse an hour after dark; again thanks to Farrell's detailed directions he had no trouble finding it. He swung the truck through the open doors of the maintenance bay. They were closed behind him immediately. As he climbed out of the cab Farrell's men were already going to work.

He watched them from a glass cubicle. A man brought him

red wine, cold meat, bread and coffee, but he kept his eyes away from Kemp's face, like the others there he wanted to know as little as necessary.

The trailer was approved for TIR which meant that once it was loaded, inspected and sealed it could cross borders without being inspected by Customs again until it reached its country of destination.

It was a scheme arranged by the United Nations, and the key to it lay in the contents of the trailer being accessible through only one door – and this sealed by Customs at the port of departure.

Seals varied from country to country. Drivers who were dishonest liked Italian seals – they were secured by string which could be cut, retied and then the knot slipped out of sight. They liked the Portuguese too – skilful men could wriggle them loose with a pin.

The seals on this trailer, though, were as thief-proof as possible – wires, secured with lead balls into which British Customs had imprinted their seal. It could be opened by cutting, but never closed again.

Kemp watched the men cut, open the doors and begin unloading the vehicle parts. He was not worried about the resealing. Farrell was organised enough to have sealing equipment and forged seals.

While men unloaded, three others were covering the company markings on the sides of the trailer with large squares of white vinyl film. These were in turn covered with a new name and the yellow shape of a running mountain lion, all cut from the same vinyl which was marketed for small truckers wanting to customise their own vehicles.

That done, the plates were changed on both the tractor and the trailer. Kemp noted that the interior was empty now, and two men carried in a small winch and securing ropes.

Finally – and it had taken well under an hour – one of the men began taking Polaroid photographs of the trailer to attach to the forged certificate attesting that the vehicle had been inspected and passed for TIR travel.

Almost immediately the men disappeared. Kemp ate the

last piece of bread and drained the coffee. He walked out to the truck, examined the outside carefully, inspected the winch inside, checked that it worked easily and tested the ropes that would secure the helicopter.

Finally satisfied, he climbed up into the cab, lay down on the bunk fully clothed, and slept. The man who had brought him food woke him at two a.m.

Inside the cubicle, under neon lights, Kemp drank more coffee and checked through the folder of documents handed him: transit permits for crossing France and Spain, TIR documents, consignments notes, a Shell fuel credit card, a goods manifest . . .

"They're all there," said the man. "Everything. You needn't worry."

Kemp nodded, but said nothing.

At two twenty a.m. on Wednesday 17 April the huge garage doors were pulled open and the Volvo truck eased out on to the N20. The cab had not warmed yet, but Kemp was hot with excitement.

The car dropped Farrell within sight of the parked helicopter just before three a.m. The driver helped unload the dozen jerricans of aviation fuel before driving away towards Marseilles.

Farrell, the cans near his feet, settled down in a clump of trees. He doubted he would need the fuel – pilots invariably refuelled at the end of the day to save time in the morning, but it was better to be safe.

Farrell studied the helicopter through nightglasses. It was about one hundred and fifty yards away and covered with a tarpaulin. He carried a small bag, and out of it he took a flask of black coffee.

He sipped, checked his watch. Small, single-engine helicopters were not suitable for night flying except with special blind-flying instruments. He had special nightglasses, though, and in any event he would wait until just before dawn – the sound of a helicopter flying overhead at night could too easily alert attention.

At three forty, taking his bag but leaving the fuel cans, he climbed a hedge and skirted the field until he reached the helicopter. He cut the ropes holding the tarpaulin, pulled it clear and tried the door. Locked, as he had expected. The fourth key he tried fitted.

Inside, he turned the master switch and checked the fuel – plenty for the distance he planned to fly. He closed the door, strapped himself in, started the engine and pulled on the rotor clutch to start the blades. The sound was frightening in the stillness.

It took only two minutes for the gauges to show that all the pressures and temperatures had reached the right level, and that the rotor speed matched the engine speed. But it seemed longer.

Finally, Farrell opened the throttle, and pulling on the collective lever the helicopter began to climb away. The sky was lightening now. Farrell's eyes scanned the ground, half expecting to see someone alerted by the noise. But there was no one.

Within thirty seconds the helicopter reached its maximum speed. He stayed low to keep off any radar screens. The land below was familiar; he had driven over it twice, studied maps with the care of a rally driver.

He had fifty miles, less than thirty minutes flight, ahead of him.

Kemp was early. He pulled back from the road at the designated spot, stopped and swung himself down from the cab, grateful for the early morning air.

There was still thirty-five minutes if Farrell were on time. He walked away from the truck, checked that nothing obstructed the field, and then unfastened the back of the trailer ready. The wire, lead and special pliers inside would enable him to fit new seals when the time came.

Nervousness made him want to defecate, but he remained near the truck, gazing into the night sky, the torch ready in his hand.

Just before four thirty he heard the sound of the helicopter.

He shone the torch three times, paused, and then kept repeating the pattern. Farrell's best landmark though would be the truck itself – the men at the garage had marked the top with a large square of fluorescent vinyl.

At four thirty-seven the helicopter touched down, gently and hesitantly at first because Farrell was not sure of the surface.

As soon as he killed the engine Farrell swung himself down, crouching under the blades. The trailer doors were already wide open.

The men nodded, but did not speak. As soon as the blades stopped turning, they manhandled the one-ton helicopter from the field on to the side road – a surprisingly easy task.

The blades took ten minutes to remove. Then Kemp fixed the rope to the craft and manned the hand winch, hauling the helicopter up the ramp and into the back of the trailer. Farrell secured the ropes.

In less than twenty minutes they were on their way. Farrell sat beside him in the co-driver's seat.

Once they were out of the area Farrell would join the helicopter in the trailer and Kemp would re-seal the doors.

They would make the border in good time for the morning Customs checks. Everything was on target.

## 18

At noon, as Singleton had pleaded, the hijackers announced that they were extending their deadline by forty-eight hours "to give the Imperialists, east and west, a final chance."

This time delivery was direct: a telephone call to the Press Association in London and another, simultaneously, to the Associated Press Bureau in Bonn. With each one there was a phrase that enabled police to confirm its authenticity.

Singleton, sweating out his inactivity in the house at the spa, received the news within a half-hour. To celebrate, he poured himself a glass of wine – the postponement was not essential but it helped. If it were on schedule – and he had no doubt that it would be – Muntwick's 'parcel' would not arrive until the next morning. And the delay meant that they could carry out the raid on Friday night, with the prison authorities more relaxed than they would have been if they thought the deadline had been reached.

The telephone rang twice more in the next half-hour, "Good, you've done well," he said in response to the first call before hanging up. To the second he listened with few comments, before saying, "I understand. I'll be there." Well over an hour before he needed to do anything. He felt so relaxed that he rifled through the kitchen, found eggs, made an omelette and drank more wine. It was only later, looking back, that he realised that he had been trying to impose normality on what was a kind of madness.

There was no problem crossing the border at Irun, only a long, boring wait because the Customs men were working to rule.

The action was because a Customs man had been killed two days before in a ETA bombing of a San Sebastián bar, and this was their protest.

One or two drivers, unfamiliar with the Spanish, were stupid enough to protest at the delays, brought by the Customs men insisting on minute scrutiny of every document carried.

Kemp, on the other hand, acted resigned but neutral – and was waved through without any trouble.

As they crossed, he jerked the truck twice – to an onlooker a piece of bad driving, but in reality a way of telling Farrell, locked in the trailer, that they were through.

Mid-morning he turned off the road and into a deserted warehouse, arranged by Farrell. Suddenly, and unexpectedly, he began to shudder as though with fever.

Neither Kate Galbraith nor Don Sobers, the FBI man on the co-ordinating committee, read Ralph Leger's round-up on the search until four days after it appeared.

Kate's copy had not long arrived by post, and she read the article because of what she knew of Singleton's involvement and because it carried Leger's byline.

Sobers read it almost by accident, the committee were receiving all the newspaper clippings, and at this particular moment he had virtually nothing else to do.

Nothing interested him until he reached the paragraph about Ross – and even then it excited him little. He imagined – rightly, as it happened – that the reporter had suspected something on small evidence, had been unable to substantiate it in any way, and had included the paragraph in the hope it would stimulate a response. If he had known anything, or had any real hopes of learning anything, he would hardly have used up the story in one tucked-away paragraph.

Nevertheless, it was enough on a quiet day to send Sobers tracking back through the files. He had read the brief FBI report by Agent Glenn Webb who had first tracked down

Ross's home address, but had not bothered to consult any of the officer's later reports.

He would go through them now. It was over two hours later and repeated checks and cross checks that Sobers accepted the fact that there were no later reports on file. Nor was there any trace of the original brief report, innocuous though it was.

Ten minutes later he tried Webb's office on the pretext he had information to give. Webb was not there. No, they had no idea when he would be back; he might be away for a time; could someone else help?

Sobers deliberated for a half hour before making his next call. He did so after convincing himself that his position on the committee would make such a call seem routine.

It was to FBI Personnel. He introduced himself and explained that he wanted to clarify some points with Agent Glenn Webb. Where could he locate him?

There was a very long pause before another voice came on the line.

They were not able to help, apologised the voice. Webb was on an assignment outside the United States and even to Sobers nothing more could be said. It was understood, though, that he had already been interviewed at length and had been able to supply nothing of any substance.

If Sobers wanted to pursue it any further, of course, he could only refer him to the Director's office.

Sobers forced himself to speak evenly. "No, what the hell," he said, "just me with too few leads raking too small. There's obviously nothing that's not already in the file. Just sorry to have troubled you."

When he replaced the receiver, though, his heart was thumping. He *knew* he had something. He didn't know what, but he knew it was important. All his instincts sharpened by years of training told him so. The only question was whether to dig a little deeper, or pass on what he knew now.

Muntwick's companies were complex to a degree that it would have taken a score of lawyers and accountants a lifetime to make any order from them.

They were registered in a dozen countries, in a hundred or more names, through a score of nominees. The result was complex, but the aim was simple – to produce the biggest tax advantages, and to make it virtually impossible for anyone to know exactly what Muntwick did and did not own.

The 212,000 ton supertanker Zeres was registered in Panama and its owners were the Kapat Corporation, with an address in Liechtenstein.

This spring it was carrying crude oil from the Persian Gulf to Rotterdam. On this particular day, the day that Kemp and Farrell crossed the border and Singleton finalised his plans, it was acting on new instructions. To slow and change course for Gironde in order to divest oil for Bordeaux.

The instructions were quite precise. Following them, the captain would have Zeres about ten miles off the north Spanish coast on the night of Friday 19 April.

It was the first time that Ross had seen the woman since the hijacking.

He had been drugged and moved again. That he knew, but he did not know how far. He could have been in the next street, the next town, the next continent.

His new home, though, was much more roomy – part, he thought from the little he could see, of an unused warehouse.

His bed was a mattress on the floor, but there was also a chair, and one of the guards had given him three old copies of *Reader's Digest*.

Most of all, though, there was even a window – small, barely a foot square. He had to stand on tip-toe to see through it, and the view was restricted: a small, paved yard, surrounded by a high brick wall that reached up so high that only a strip of grey sky was visible.

But it was more than enough to raise his spirits.

In his old prison, before the move, he had found himself reliving parts of his life despite attempts not to do so.

*Reader's Digest*, he thought wryly, could have made something of it – if only he had turned out to be a statesman or Nobel prize-winning scientist. His mother had died in childbirth; his father had been killed in World War II when he was nine.

Neither of those happenings seemed real, although no doubt they had affected his life. They were too far back.

What he could remember vividly was his uncle and aunt who had brought him up on their small homestead in the Mid-West. They had belonged to some strange religious sect, so special that it was said there were but a few thousand worldwide who believed and would, thus, be saved.

In practice, it had seemed to involve the following of every taboo and restriction of every other religion combined. This God was an unsmiling, unforgiving, demanding, funless deity. The idea of hell had been forced constantly into Ross, but there were times that he doubted the devil who lived there could be worse than his uncle and aunt's God in heaven.

At twenty, weak and pressured, he had married an eighteen-year-old girl, a neighbour's daughter, another of the faith. Everyone, including him, had been surprised when she left seven weeks later and had made, so rumour said, for New York.

He too had left then, stealing away in the night to escape the protests and the emotional outpourings. He had not been back since. Nor had he ever written.

For almost twenty years he had drifted, doing nothing, doing everything, earning just enough but not caring because there was little he wanted.

He was not homosexual – when he was forced to think about it he concluded he was really nothing; his sexual feelings were almost nonexistent – but it was a man, another drifter, who had talked him into trying to better himself.

For a time he had tried everything – Carnegie courses, Meditation, Therapy, Yoga . . . But it was computer programming that had saved him. On impulse he had taken an aptitude test, had been persuaded he was 'perfect', and not knowing this was the answer given to everyone had signed up on an expensive course which he paid for by working in a bar twelve hours a night. And, surprisingly, he had been good.

And in being good, and being known to be so, he had found a place in life.

Then the hijacking and the return of the fears.

But with the move to the new prison he felt better. A kidnapped man endures a variety of barely endurable shocks: lack of privacy, solitary confinement, discomfort, inactivity . . . If those were not enough, there was the constant fear of the unknown.

But suddenly Ross had become convinced that he could survive. He had discovered prayer, not the harsh incantations of the days with his uncle and aunt, but the gentler, more childish requests of his boyhood. He was, he thought, stronger. He had come through the worst part.

This new room helped. All it had in common with the last one was the bare bulb, again high and out of reach. But with a window it did not draw him so much.

His guards helped too. There were again two of them, but these actually used names – Kurt and Helmut. They communicated little, but they were not antagonistic – the magazines were proof of that.

And he had almost forgotten the woman.

He saw her first as he stared out of the window, delighting in the simple pleasure of the patterns that the sun made on the red-brick wall.

She walked into his view, her back towards him, and began to attach a piece of rope between two walls. On it, still with her back towards him, she hung a shirt, a brassière, and two pairs of pants to dry.

She turned and he realised what he must have known but not registered: that she was naked from the waist. Her breasts were elongated, lemon shaped, and very white against the brown of the rest of her body. She lifted her arms, and her breasts were raised.

She stood like that for a long time, her eyes raised upwards. Then she placed her hands under her breasts, cupped them, and began slowly, to stroke the undersides, slowing her touch as she reached the nipples.

Still her eyes were upwards. But Ross knew she knew he

was watching. Suddenly she stopped, stared direct at his window, and then was gone.

He sat on the edge of the bed taut, quivering with a strange, not pleasant feeling. He knew something would happen.

He lifted his head as he heard the bolt drawn, but did not stand. She was alone. She had pulled on a sweater under which her nipples jutted. She was dressed completely in black, from the ski pants to a scarf she had tied around her hair. She had a pistol in her hand, and she stood, the free hand on her hip, mouth twisted in a smile, a still almost from a porn magazine. Then slowly she lifted the pistol until it was pointed at his head.

Her smile became broader, and Ross, mesmerised, began to sweat.

Then she pulled the trigger.

There was a click in the silent room. The pin had hit an empty chamber.

"Just practising," said the woman. "You know you've little time left."

She backed out of the room, her face still fixed in a smile.

Ross stared at the door, and realised there were tears streaming down his face.

The town, a dozen miles inland, was ugly and industrialised. Late Wednesday, Singleton drove along the lines of prefabricated factory units and turned left towards the bullring. The streets were quiet. The fights – part of the celebrations of the town's saint – were well under way.

The meeting had been arranged as a result of his brief initial conversation with the Basque in the Santander café.

Two men were waiting for him. One of them, also a Basque, led him to a seat on the cheap, sunny side of the ring. The men on either side of him had wax paper cups of beer; one wore a paper visor even though by now – the fifth bull of the afternoon – the sun was losing its strength.

"You know the bull fight?" said the man with the visor, without turning his head. "It is time for the kill. What we call the *hora de la verdad*. The bull has been . . ." He groped for a word . . . "punished. Now he will be killed."

He turned to face Singleton. The man on the American's other side stared impassively ahead. "You will tell me what you want," he said.

Singleton wore a shoulder bag – the kind tourists pack with cameras and personal belongings. "When I leave," he said, "I want you to take this, to arrange its delivery."

"What is in it?"

"Plastic. They will need it to get to the yard."

"We have plastic. There was no need."

"I wanted to be sure. This is good stuff."

"And?"

"There are some pills. They should each take one about an hour before. We may have to use gases. These will act as an antidote. It should be made clear to them they *must* take them."

"Shhhh."

The Spaniard's attention had returned to the ring. The matador had lifted the *muletta* high, checking whether the bull followed its motion. Satisfied, he turned his body, flipped the *muletta* over the end of the short wooden stick, the *palillo*, sighted down his sword, bounced on his toes and charged. The bull moved too.

There was a swell of pent-up excitement from the crowd.

The sword struck home. Moments later, blood began to gush from the bull's mouth.

Peons ran out and began to spin the bull by waving capes on alternating sides. "A bad kill," said the Spaniard, rising and drawing Singleton with him. "The sword was deflected by the spine, hit the lungs. What they're doing now to wear him down is illegal, but it's done all the time."

He led Singleton to the back of the plaza, and took the bag from him.

"What else?" he said. "Tell me the timings."

Singleton did.

"Very well. It will all be done."

"There will be no problems?"

"No, access isn't a worry."

Both men still stared towards the ring. The spectators were booing now. The bull was still spinning, still belching blood.

"There's one more thing," said Singleton. "The man you have who has access to the prisoners. Can he come and go much as he pleases?"

The Spaniard stared at Singleton, considering the question carefully before replying. "Pretty much so," he said at last. "He is with the civil police. He liaises on security with the prison."

"He is a sympathiser?"

The Spaniard snorted disparagingly. "Money," he said. "The man is a pig. He does it for money. But he's useful."

"I'll need to know how to make contact with him direct if necessary," said Singleton.

The Spaniard turned, surprised. "No. No," he said. "That cannot be done."

"Look," said Singleton. "We have forty-eight hours to go, a complex plan that relies on careful timing. What if we have to make changes at the last moment? Say we are delayed a half-hour and those inside do not know? What do they do? Stand in the yard, saying to the warders 'Please don't shoot us, our rescuers are late?'"

A long pause. In the ring the bull was on his knees.

"You would only use contact in such an emergency?"

"Of course."

"All right." The Spaniard gave him a name and a telephone number.

Singleton, face impassive, turned back to the ring. The bull was finally dead, his spinal cord cut with a dagger.

Kemp lay on his stomach in the stubbly grass. He was dressed completely in black, his head and face covered with a black stocking mask with slits for his eyes and mouth.

The road was some two hundred yards behind him, and the prison almost one hundred and fifty yards ahead. It was dark now but he studied the parts that were not floodlit through the nightscope – the telescopic device that, by intensifying ambient light, made it possible to see objects that the dark made invisible to the naked eye.

He had three main concerns. The first was somewhere to make his stance on the night, and he thought he had found that. The cover was not perfect, but it was enough.

The second was the watchtower – the only one that would have a clear coverage of the helicopter as it swept in. It had to be put out of action.

The third took him several minutes to find, even though he had studied it in photographs and on plans. The intake for the prison's air conditioning unit – vital because so much was underground. It was, he noted with relief, larger than the photographs had suggested – a good three feet by two feet. At this range, one hundred and fifty yards, he should be able to hit it every time.

He had Singleton's assurance that the air conditioning was that and no more, that it was not fitted with all the complex and expensive extras that would make it immune to chemical attack.

He lay for a long time, calculating angles and distances, checking the timing of patrols, before sliding off into the darkness.

Behind the decision there were hours of talks, of Presidential soul-searching, of mental debates of the cases for and against the action.

But at eleven thirty-five p.m. local time when the call reached Singleton at his cabin at the spa it was as spare and as direct as it could be.

For extra safety, it was scrambled and coded. Deciphered, it said simply: 'Send in the Lions.'

# 19

The container arrived by air during the middle of the morning.

It was clearly marked with the international symbol and was collected by the resident doctor from the spa. Officials examined the documents carefully. All were in order. One Customs man was visibly relieved when it was removed; despite everything he knew, he hated being near it.

Two hours later it took two men to carry it into Singleton's cabin. The doctor was the only man who realised the container's significance and he said nothing. It was not only that he had learned to do exactly what Muntwick wanted and no more, but he also suspected that the billionaire had been told something by his American doctors and the container had been delivered in that light . . .

Even the fact that it went to the cabin and not the clinic did not surprise him: Muntwick obviously wanted it somewhere where no one would see it.

Singleton waited until he was alone before working loose the elaborate safety catch. It was made harder by the fact that he wore gloves. Beside it was a bottle of brandy and he uncorked that and drained a good two inches in one gulp. The raw liquid burned his throat and stomach. He drank more.

Then, his hands trembling, he removed the stopper of the container, reached deep down inside with a long pair of forceps and gently withdrew the small bottle that lay there.

He pulled the mask up around his mouth before pouring the contents, very carefully, into the brandy bottle.

Afterwards, sweating, he sat in an adjoining room. He closed his eyes, saw the six-year-old who had been blown apart, and began to breathe deeply. Very gradually he began to stop trembling.

Ross lay on his bed, gazing up at the bare lightbulb in the ceiling. It drew him. Again it represented his captivity.

He had stopped shaking and was composed again. Until he saw the woman he thought he had come to terms with whatever might happen.

But her reappearance had resurrected all the fears, all the demons. What he feared most was not dying – but the *way* she might kill him.

He had heard of people being shot in many places before being killed. Would she do that to him? He closed his eyes and remembered the click as she had pulled the trigger.

Although frightened, he knew now that he would not talk. He had thought a lot about his secret. He had always known that he had been invited to join Vibart because of the programming he had done for Charlton. Charlton's discovery must have national importance. Otherwise there would have been publication in one of the scientific journals. Instead, silence.

Ross thought he knew the reason. He too had read the articles about trapdoor ciphers. He suspected that the United States had, in fact, been utilising them for secret transmissions and wanted the fact of Charlton's discoveries kept secret until they could replace such ciphers.

If so, it was a secret worth telling. But he would not.

Or would he? What would he do with the gun trained on him? Even more so, what would he do seconds later if he lay on the floor, conscious but with a bullet in his leg or his arm or his stomach? What would he say? Would he really remain silent?

Ross made his decision.

It was hard carrying it out. He had to roll the mattress, wedge it against the wall, and balance the chair on top of it. Then, because it was not high enough, he had to place the upturned bucket on the chair.

He fell twice and had to rebuild his makeshift stepladder.

Finally, he had to accept that no matter what he did his hands could not reach the bulb to unscrew it.

It took a further half hour to prise a lump of plaster from the wall and at the end his fingers were bleeding.

With the plaster in his hand, he climbed the rickety pile again. It swayed perilously.

On the second attempt, the bulb shattered into a score of pieces. Ross plunged his fingertips into the live socket.

Singleton sipped his beer and watched the civil guard enter the bar.

The man was in off-duty clothes, but he was exactly the way he had been described. He looked around for a few seconds and then joined Singleton.

"This is dangerous," he began. "I hope it is necessary."

Singleton had a plastic shopping bag on the table in front of him – the sign the guard had been instructed to seek.

Singleton raised his hand for the waiter, ordered another beer and then gestured to the bag.

"There's a bottle of brandy in there," he said. "I want you to deliver it, to make sure they drink it." He gazed into the policeman's querulous eyes. "You know what's planned," he said. "I want them to have it tomorrow evening." His voice became conspiratorial. "I am afraid that they will panic," he said. "The brandy has something in it – a tranquilliser . . . something to keep them calm."

The drinks arrived. The policeman lifted his glass and then said, "I'm taking enough risks already. Another is not worthwhile."

Without changing his tone, Singleton continued, "There's a hundred thousand pesetas in there too." The policeman could not hide his reaction. More money than he had ever dreamed about.

"Do what I ask you," said Singleton, "and it is yours." He stared into the policeman's face. "And there will be another hundred thousand," he added. He pushed the bag across the table. "Just one thing," he added quietly. "You tell no one. And if it isn't done, rest assured that I will know."

## 20

The launch belonged to the spa and was frequently taken out for fishing trips. Normally there was a professional captain but on Thursday evening Singleton took it out alone. The fact that he was Muntwick's personal guest was enough to prevent protests.

It was some years since Singleton had been out to sea alone – once sailing had been a passion. But this was an easy boat to handle, and he remembered all his navigation. He had no doubt that he would be in place at the right time.

Kemp had spent the day trying to relax, utilising all his Yoga training. After the raid on the prison, Singleton, Farrell and the freed terrorists would all escape in Muntwick's tanker, with which they had a rendezvous ten miles off the coast. Kemp, though, would have to try to get out by land, helped by the two Basques who would await his return to the warehouse. Even if everything went well, it could be some days before he slept again.

Darkness, though, was a relief. Again, he dressed completely in black. A car dropped him as near to the prison as was safe, and he made his way cautiously until he was one hundred and fifty yards from the building.

He slid flat on to the ground and opened the black hold-all that he had carried so carefully. In it was the crossbow he had brought out from England, light in weight, only eight pounds, but with a draw strength of 220 pounds to help accuracy in casting the specially made heavy bolts which Singleton had obtained via Muntwick.

A normal rifle-type gas grenade launcher would not give him the accuracy he needed at this range – apart from the noise. The bow was already fitted with a nightscope. He laid it beside him together with the bolts themselves – a dozen, more than he would need. They were eighteen inches long, longer than normal for crossbow bolts. But the extra length helped distribute the extra weight of the cylindrical cannister engineered in at the point end. Kemp knew that, within reason, the weight of the bolt was not the problem; it was retaining its balance.

Most of the cannister, like the rest of the bolt, was made of aluminium. The end of it – where the point of the bolt would normally be – was an inch length of glass.

On the other side of the bow there was a lever to help him cock the mechanism after firing each bolt. Without such aid, it would be impossible to pull such a heavy draw weight.

The last item to be removed from the bag was a Heckler and Koch sniper rifle, fitted too with nightscope and silencer.

He would try dropping one of the bolts into the watch-tower that so threatened Farrell on his approach and take-off. But it was a chancy shot. If the first missed he would transfer to the rifle.

There was still almost an hour to go – the raid was timed for three a.m. Nevertheless, he double-checked the range, set the sights on the bow, then stretched out to wait. He was absolutely relaxed now.

Singleton, too, was in position. The radio had picked up the coded message from the tanker. At three fifteen a.m., the time Farrell would drop the helicopter in the sea near the launch, it should be passing about three miles further out, almost stopped. The night was cold and dark and Singleton, gazing out into the blackness from the rail, shivered, turned up his collar and for a moment wished he was back bird-watching beside the Potomac.

* * *

At two thirty a.m. Rafael Lopez retreated further back into the watchtower and carefully lit a cigarette which he would smoke behind cupped fingers.

He stumbled over Ortiz's foot and quietly cursed the drunk and sleeping man who lay at his feet. Antonio Ortiz was the guard he had relieved at midnight. Ortiz was also his brother-in-law, and Lopez had helped get him his job.

Ortiz should have climbed down from the tower, gone home. But instead he had stayed, hidden from below by the chest-high stone walls, seated in a corner, telling Lopez, quietly but passionately that his wife had gone away to tend a girlfriend who was ill. Really, it emerged, he was convinced she was having an affair. He had already been drinking from the bottle he had hidden on him. As he talked, he drank more, finally falling into a drunk sleep. Lopez, though afraid they would be discovered, had tolerated Ortiz's dangerous presence, because he knew the man was right. She was having an affair. Many people knew and as her brother it shamed him. Nevertheless he would confess no knowledge to Ortiz; the man was a milksop, unable to cope with his own woman. Reluctantly, though, he himself would do something. In time.

The helicopter was ready for take-off. Farrell had stripped every item that was not essential for flight. The items he had added were of insignificant weight – the tiny radio receiver that would enable him to home-in accurately on Singleton, although there were precise navigational directions. And the small explosive charge that would destroy the helicopter once he and the others had transferred to the launch, making it look as though the craft had crashed, destroying its occupants.

It was a way of adding vital extra breathing space to enable them to reach the tanker.

The two Basque terrorists who would look after Kemp helped him wheel the helicopter out of the warehouse into the concrete, enclosed yard.

Two forty-nine. Nine minutes to take-off. It was all carefully calculated – less than two minutes to reach the prison, a minute to land, load and take-off, between ten and fifteen minutes to reach the launch. With luck – and the diversions – they would be well hidden aboard the tanker before anyone realised enough of what was happening to be able to do anything that would endanger the operation.

Kemp had already slid the first bolt into the bow. It was twenty minutes to three.

The sights were set and the string was already cocked. He needed to land eight bolts on target – he should, he was sure, be able to achieve that by firing ten of the twelve bolts. There was a crosswind, but it was light, and, in any event, the extra heavy weight of the bolts minimised its effect.

Even using the lever to help him cock the bow, he knew he could comfortably keep up a firing rate of two bolts a minute. Five minutes at most.

The square shape of the intake for the air conditioning projected from the roof of the prison, silhouetted against the skyline. Kemp centred it carefully in his sights. He wriggled to get himself comfortable and then eased off the safety catch.

At two forty-five Kemp squeezed the trigger and watched impassive as the bolt left the bow at 300 feet per second, a fifth of the speed of a bullet leaving a hunting rifle.

It hit the air intake low, at a seven o'clock position. Despite his elation, Kemp recocked the bow and reached out for a second bolt. He knew what was happening, although he could see nothing. The glass at the front of the bolt would be shattering on impact, and the gas would be sucked into the air conditioning, to be fully circulated within a matter of minutes.

It was KQ gas – the successor to BZ. Although stockpiled and made in large quantities by the military and commercial arms manufacturers, it had been used in the field only once, and then the outcry had been so great that it had been shifted into storage.

KQ acted quickly – within seconds. Its inventors claimed that it was humane, that its long-term effects – on healthy people admittedly – were nil. But short-term it produced a high fever – the recipient felt as though he would actually burst with the heat. And if that was not enough, there was the highly increased heart rate, the tight pains across the chest, the double vision and the terrible feeling of imminent catastrophe. In all, a terrible gas.

By three a.m. it was being emitted in every room, every cell, in the prison, except inside one small block where the terrorists, on instructions, had blocked all the air vents.

And at precisely the same time Kemp heard the helicopter, high in the night sky, as it zoomed towards him.

Below him the ground looked as though it was bathed in moonlight thanks to the nightscope glasses.

The prison itself, when it came into view within a minute or so, was illuminated by its own floodlights. Farrell was flying at 400 feet and full speed and he began to drop fast as he saw the mark – a white sheet – that the prisoners had placed in the small exercise yard moments before.

The sheet marked the centre of the yard – an essential help if he was going to land and then take off again in the restricted space, without smashing the rotor blades into the surrounding walls.

There was little time to think, but he found himself hoping that Kemp had done his job well. If there was gunfire, he was doomed. His margins for error were too slight.

At forty feet, the yard immmediately below, he saw a guard in a tower aim his rifle. He was concentrating on the mechanics of flying too much to get emotional. It did not even register when the guard shot backwards, threw his arms in the air letting his gun fall to the ground. A greater reality was the ground rushing up to meet him.

They were crouched in the corner of the small yard, the air full of the smell of the explosion where they had blasted through the tunnel minutes before.

The Irishman, Flynn, was breathing deeply, trying to be

calm but nervous because he alone of the terrorists had inhaled some of the gas. Despite their precautions a thin spiral of the white vapour had seeped through the vent. The nearest, he had rushed forward to plug the gap with a piece of cloth torn from his shirt. He convinced himself that the antidote pill he had taken would counteract any effects.

Then the helicopter was swooping down, and the need to act killed all other thoughts.

They began running towards it the moment it landed, a single line, only paces between them, each ducked low under the whirring blades.

The pilot was shouting instructions but his words were lost in the roar of the engines.

Flynn was last to reach the doorway. The helicopter was already beginning to lift away and he threw himself forwards. His hand grasped a piece of metal and then, moist with his fear, started to slip.

Titov, the Ukrainian, tried to grab him, but Flynn fell.

The skid halted his fall and he threw his arms around it.

The helicopter lurched and then soared upwards, Flynn clinging on below, his feet kicking in the air.

Kemp had watched the guard stagger and fall. He had not even tried sending a bolt into the tower to incapacitate the man with gas. There had not been time. Nevertheless, he hoped he had not killed him – he had aimed for the shoulder, fairly certain that the shock of the unjacketed bullet as it expanded on impact would be enough to put the man out of action.

When his eyes dropped to the yard walls the helicopter was already beginning to rise again. It was all going to plan.

It was not the fall of his brother-in-law, nor the screams from the prison yard, that woke Ortiz. It was simply a desire to be violently sick.

He staggered to his feet and took two steps forward before he realised where he was. Then he saw the shape of Lopez, half huddled against the wall. Suddenly partially sober, he bent and reached out his hand. It came away covered with blood.

The whirring noise outside drew him back to the view out over the prison. A helicopter, almost drunken in its lurching, was pulling into the sky.

Ortiz was not a good guard, but he knew what he had to do. He stumbled forward, took the gun from the floor, and began spraying bullets into the air.

He was too drunk to aim well, but quantity was enough. In the comparative quiet of the night, he could hear shots ricochet off the craft.

For a heady, glorious, exciting minute or two Farrell was sure it was all right. Six men were inside, another was hanging on to the skids. But they were out. Safe.

Then he felt the twist grip of the throttle jam – it would scarcely turn back and forth. A bullet must have jammed in the system, cutting power. Unless he did something they would just lose height.

There was no chance, with seven men as passengers, of reaching the launch.

# 21

The firing had stopped. Farrell, struggling to consider possibilities, cursed Kemp: the man should have shot the guard earlier; he had obviously delayed.

The helicopter was flying – but, with only half the engine power, barely so. It would not climb and its speed was dangerously low. The men crowded in beside him were murmuring in fear: it was obvious something was wrong.

Below, Farrell could see one man clinging on to one of the skids, and briefly he toyed with the idea of pulling the helicopter into a sharp turn in the hope of throwing the man free. Immediately, he realised that the loss in weight would make little positive difference. With so many on board, the helicopter had only a minute or two's flying time.

The answer was obvious, but he made the decision with reluctance. He turned back, away from the sea, and towards the warehouse he had left only minutes before.

As he came down, the helicopter rolling drunkenly, he saw the two Basques rushing out to meet them. He tried to hover for a few seconds so that the man who had been on the skids could slide down but the lack of power was so great that the craft hit the ground hard.

"Out! Out!" Farrell had to start pushing the men despite the force of his voice.

He could see the man who had been on the skid – he had been thrown clear and was being helped to his feet. He looked unhurt.

Above the flap of the rotors and the whine of the engine, he heard a voice – "What the fuck's happening?"

"Out!" he screamed again. There was no time to explain anything. He had to lash the last man across the face to make him jump down. He looked out on one of the Basques – "No power," he yelled. "You'll have to try to get them away. I'll try and make a diversion."

Even without the seven men's weight the helicopter would not rise at first. He drove it across the concrete, like a car, out through the open gates on to the road and gradually, inch by inch, managed to edge it into the air.

It took almost five minutes to reach one hundred feet, and at that height he levelled and headed out for sea. He was about five miles out, half the distance, when the gauge suddenly registered nil pressure.

It was, he knew, the end.

Instinctively, he began to carry out the procedure to 'autorote' – what every helicopter pilot knows how to do if the engine stops. He dumped the collective lever to put the rotors into fine pitch so that they would turn faster. Then, as the sea loomed nearer, he pulled the blades into course pitch to reverse the airflow and cushion the ditching.

At the last moment he unbuckled his strap and rolled in the direction of the door – there was no need to open it: as a weight saver it had been removed.

Even with all this, he remembered to pull the pin on the four-minute time fuse.

His plans, once he hit the water, were vague – probably start swimming in the direction of land, hoping that the explosion would persuade anyone searching that there were no survivors.

With the upholstery torn out to save weight, the seats were a skeleton of metal rods. Farrell's jacket was embedded in one as he tried to dive through the door. The helicopter was already down, deceptively evenly balanced almost as though it had made a normal landing.

Knowing he had minutes to spare, Farrell was not afraid. He reached out and began to tug himself loose. At that moment the helicopter tilted violently in the sea, sending him skidding head first across the cabin. The blow did not quite knock him unconscious. But it was enough to leave him dazed until the explosion ripped the helicopter into a thousand pieces.

Singleton never saw the helicopter. But he heard it.

There was something in the sound that made him nervous that something might not be right. But it was only in the last seconds – the silence and then the two explosions – that he realised how bad it was.

Despite the obvious dangers, he steered the launch in the direction of the crash, but, not surprisingly, could find nothing.

Finally, he turned his attention to the radio beam from the tanker and headed towards it.

Half an hour later he was hauled aboard. Before he went he smashed open holes in the launch – it would be underwater within minutes.

On board, there were no questions. He was led to a cabin where there were fresh clothes. He dressed in the outfit that was waiting for him, and only then was he conscious of the captain and the other changes of clothing.

"They're not coming," he said flatly.

He took the glass of rum that the captain pushed into his hand, and stared at the wall.

Farrell and the seven men all dead. All at the bottom of the sea. A total waste of lives and time.

# 22

The sound of Ross's body hitting the floor brought in the two guards, pistols in their hands.

"Bring a light," Kurt shouted. There was a smell of burned flesh. When the lamp arrived, they could see that one hand was blackened.

"Is he dead?" Ross's body was twisted and his mouth was open and his features contorted.

"If not, let the bastard die." The voice was the girl's. She had just entered the room.

Helmut, though, began giving Ross heart massage and mouth to mouth resuscitation.

"It's beating!" he exclaimed after a few moments. Ross's chest began to rise and fall by itself.

"Will he live?"

"How the shit should I know? Get Braun."

Twenty minutes later Ross, whose body had been twitching, was lying on the bed sedated.

Braun – a doctor – was matter-of-fact. "He'll live," he said. "Ideally, though, he ought to be taken to hospital . . ."

"No hospital."

Braun had expected the reply. "I just thought I should say it." He took some tablets from his medical bag. "He'll be in pain. Feed him these."

As he closed his bag and stood ready to leave, he heard the one woman in the room mutter, "I still think we should have let the bastard die."

It was four days before the captain put Singleton, equipped with false papers, ashore at Rotterdam.

Singleton had remained alone in his cabin. There had been constant coded messages from Muntwick – ones he alone could decypher. But after the first day he had simply tossed them aside uncoded and not bothered to reply. There was a limit to the amount of abuse he could take.

The captain was glad to see him go. Singleton, eyes unseeing, asked a cab driver to take him to a hotel, any hotel. An hour later, inside a poky room, he fell asleep, fully clothed and very drunk.

Sobers had nursed his secret about Ross and the 'missing' FBI man Glenn Webb for almost a week.

In the end, personal ambition had won. If he handed over the raw information he had, it might or might not be helpful, but he had doubts over whether it would advance his own position much. Someone else, after all, would have to find out whether it meant something or nothing.

If, on the other hand, Sobers could keep quiet, pursue the lead himself, and come up with something concrete, it would mean a lot.

Sobers was a Soviet agent, first and foremost, because he was being blackmailed for a sexual relationship (long past) with an under-age girl. He suspected it was KGB-arranged but could never know.

Once he had begun to co-operate, however, a secondary reason had taken over – money. The Soviets had quickly found he was a greedy man, best operated if he were paid by results.

The hope of big results – and, thus, big money – made him delay this time.

But events began to move too fast. Once the terrorists were free, he knew time was running out. If he didn't pass on information now, slight though it was, he risked earning nothing.

At eight five p.m., the exact scheduled time if he wanted to call a meeting, he dialled the number from a pay telephone, engaged in a seemingly innocuous conversation with a man called Larry, and then went home.

He had arranged for a meeting with his Soviet controller the following evening. He had not wanted to make it urgent –

it would give him another twenty-four hours to try to add to his information. If he was unable to do so, he would settle for what he had got, telling his controller he had only just learned it.

The newspaper belonged to the large Dutchman at the next table and Singleton found it hard to focus through his hangover.

A half-hour later, though, he found a news-stand selling English newspapers and bought the *Daily Mail*.

The story occupied most of the front page, and much of that was a photograph – the seven terrorists who had been in jail in Spain.

The article, Singleton read, was by a Belgian journalist who had been kidnapped, blindfolded, driven around for countless hours, and then confronted by the men.

They had posed for photographs and then had answered some of the journalist's questions.

They had been moved out of Spain via the border with France with the help of sympathisers and the use of 'well established routes'. They confirmed something which, apparently, had already been reported at length, that their rescuers were the Concorde hijackers. They refused to reveal whether they had made any contact with those kidnappers.

The article went on to fill in some of the background – Singleton was able to read of his own involvement in the plot, finding himself wrongly linked with the hijackers and not Muntwick. And there was the revelation that he had been drowned when his launch went down somewhere off the Spanish coast.

He found a phone and called the nearest of the numbers that Warren had given him. Paris.

"I'm in Rotterdam," he said.

The voice was impassive. "Call again in one hour."

He did. This time there were instructions. "The view from the Euromast tower is quite spectacular."

The man in the black blazer and yellow tie picked him up there an hour later. He had been waiting.

They left together, took the escalator down to the tunnel that ran for over a mile under the River Maas and talked in the little garden on the far side.

A car took him to the hotel, and it was there late the same night that he talked with Warren.

"You took a long time calling," reprimanded Warren.

They were sitting in Singleton's hotel room, drinking warm scotch out of toothmugs taken from the bathroom.

The lie came smoothly. "There was nothing I could do until I was back on land."

Warren stared hard at him. He had flown over, taking an obvious risk, because of his fears. "You're okay, George?" he asked. "It's been a rough one, Farrell's death and that. You'd tell me if you were cracking."

"I'm all right."

"Okay. That's good. It's *you* they want to see."

Singleton listened to the instructions as given to the telephone contact point. The hijackers, satisfied, were willing to hand over their captives. He was to go to Frankfurt, book into the Intercontinental and wait for instructions.

Singleton was incredulous. "They've got their men," he said. "Why bother to go through with their end of the deal?"

"There's still the money. Besides, maybe they've realised that they need to operate by some kind of rules. This isn't going to be the last time. Even between enemies there's got to be some kind of trust – goddammit, we and the Russians learned that a long time ago. We're out there fighting, but we don't kill each other's agents. We've learned it would be self-defeating."

"When do I go?"

"I'd say tonight."

"Okay."

Warren smiled. "You look pretty good for a dead man," he said.

Sobers' controller, a middle-aged first secretary at the Soviet Embassy in Washington, had been under increasing pressure for information since the moment news of the original hijacking reached Moscow.

Demands had increased dramatically since the prison break, and because of this and because, like all good KGB men who want to survive, he notified the Moscow Centre in a coded radio message that he was keeping a meeting requested by Sobers.

The message contained his own code number and Sobers's code name, *Hawkeye*.

Because the message contained a priority number, signifying its urgency, which was already known to NSA intercepting machinery, attempts to break it began immediately.

It was in trapdoor cipher and within a little over an hour it yielded enough of its secrets for the code-breakers to know the sender and that an urgent meeting with one of the sender's agents was scheduled to take place.

Who he was due to meet, when and where was not known. But within less than an hour more, the first secretary had been located and a massive surveillance operation, of men and equipment, was under way.

Singleton had fifteen minutes to wait at the airport, and he spent ten of them debating whether he should telephone Kate.

He doubted whether she had heard anything yet, but soon, he thought, there would be news that he was presumed dead.

Telephoning her would be out of keeping – but so had been their last meeting. He would not say much; just that he was all right, and that she should not believe anything she heard in the next few days.

By the time he decided he would call, though, it was too late – there was a line of people waiting to make international calls.

A half-hour later he was glad; it probably was best not to call her. At least, not yet.

The bar was on M Street near 19th and the Russian entered feeling as relaxed as you could be at a time like this.

He had left home nearly two hours before, had rapidly decided he was being followed, which was not unusual, but was sure he had shaken his tail after an hour.

Nevertheless, he had carried out two more manoeuvres just to be sure. Now, he was convinced, he was alone.

Sobers was at the far end of the bar, halfway through a beer. He turned his head imperceptively as the Russian entered but seemingly paid no more attention as the newcomer ordered a bourbon, drank, paid and left.

Outside Sobers followed him across the street, watched him slide into his car. At the last moment, after quick glances around, Sobers ran and threw himself into the passenger seat.

The car had made less than a block before the FBI cars boxed it, dragged out the occupants, separated them, and drove them away – an operation that had taken little over two minutes.

Two of the arresting agents who had recognised Sobers were given lectures on the need for total secrecy.

The decision as to what to do with the Russian and Sobers could be taken neither by Warren nor the Director of the FBI.

It was one for the President himself, approached through Watson.

He was brief. "Lose them," he said.

Singleton's room was on the sixteenth floor and he had to wait two days before he received a call. It directed him to a *Molkerei* – a dairy shop – where he found his contact drinking a glass of milk and eating a piece of cheese.

"How long to arrange the money?" asked the contact.

"Twenty-four hours at most. You just have to tell me where."

The man did.

He finished his milk in a gulp and left Singleton seated. "Do it," he said. "We'll be in touch."

Gozori was also in Germany, but fourteen miles outside Frankfurt.

He was staying at Königstein im Taumus, a favourite weekend spot, flanked by woods and mountains. At night he could look from his hotel room at the floodlit ruins of the castle.

Like Singleton, he sat and waited.

Ross suddenly knew that everything was going to be all right.

He became conscious after his suicide attempt, at first unable to remember much and then doubly apprehensive. But his guards had been kinder than ever before – at one meal Kurt even gave him a paper cup of wine.

It seemed no more than a progression of the more humane treatment when he was moved into a much larger room one morning. Suddenly he *knew* it was nearly over. He was going to be released.

Singleton did not dare leave his room for more than minutes at a time.

The money – seven suitcases full of it – was in place, in the trunk of a car parked at the airport.

He ate meals in the room, watched a lot of television, and cleaned the gun he had been given much more than was necessary. It was not his beloved Browning, but it was a reasonable substitute, a 7.65 mm FN pistol that would give good stopping power if he needed to use it.

The message when it arrived was tucked under the plate on his breakfast tray. "Stand outside the Hotel Room Reservation Centre at the Railway Terminal," it said. It gave no time, and he left immediately.

The girl picked him up there fifteen minutes after he arrived; they took a train to Wiesbaden and returned almost immediately. This time there was a car to pick them up. Singleton sat in the back with the girl. There was no attempt to stop him following the car's route.

Singleton had once carried out an assignment in Frankfurt and he recognised the destination when the car turned off the road and into a small warehouse. It was Höchst, the city's furthest western suburb, once a town in its own right, now an industrial quarter and site of the largest chemical plant in Germany.

As he stepped out of the car he breathed in the strong smell of shoe dyes.

Four of the hostages were slumped against a wall in an inner room, watched over by two men and a girl, all of them masked. At first, he thought the prisoners were dead. No one stopped him walking over to them. Then he realised they were drugged.

"The money," said one hijacker. "Where is it?"

Singleton told him, and the man used a telephone.

"Where's the fifth hostage?" said Singleton. "The deal was for all of them."

The man shrugged. "He tried to electrocute himself. He's all right, but he's on the bed next door. You'll see him in due course."

Singleton began to move, but the gun stopped him.

It was almost an hour before the telephone rang. During the time Singleton tried to memorise everything he could about the three terrorists. They were all dressed in trousers and loose-fitting sweaters that made it difficult to judge their build, and their heads were covered with knitted helmets.

But there were things that couldn't be hidden: their heights, the way they moved, the thickness of their wrists, the colour of a few strands of hair that straggled out of the side of one mask . . .

Singleton noted them all. The girl, he had already decided, could easily be one of the three hijackers: what he could see, including her height, matched the description.

The telephone interrupted his thoughts. The man who answered listened, grunted and replaced the receiver.

"They're yours," he said. "But don't leave the building for thirty minutes. You've a watch?" Singleton nodded, and the gunman continued, "We'll have someone outside, and anyone leaving within that time will be shot."

Singleton waited until the three terrorists had been gone for five minutes. There was no rush now. He was surprised they had not searched him. But what danger was he now?

He walked through into the adjoining room, and although some instinct had partially prepared him he had to fight hard not to retch.

Ross – he supposed it was him – was literally nailed to the wooden wall in a Maltese Cross, great industrial staples thrust through his hands.

He was stripped bare and his body was a mass of blood. Nevertheless, it was possible to make out the holes – Singleton estimated he had been shot at least a dozen times, not once in any place which would have led to his immediate death.

Singleton stood transfixed, unable to move, unable to turn his eyes from the obscene sight. The rest of the room was in near darkness, there was no window in this walled-off part of the warehouse and the only light came from an industrial inspection lamp clamped on to the back of a chair near Ross's body, the bulb directed so that it illuminated the man's face. There was absolute silence.

Reluctantly, forcing himself to move, Singleton reached out to touch the body. The blood was still warm. Singleton lifted his hand and stared at the redness on his fingertips. Then, astonishingly, there was a choked gurgle. Ross was still alive!

Conflicting emotions flooded Singleton's mind: lift the body down, give Ross the kiss of life . . . turn and leave the room and come back when the man was dead for surely nothing could save him now . . . use his gun and give the man peaceful death . . .

But there was only one thing to do. He knew it, but he hesitated for a long time.

At last he reached out. During his life he had done many terrible things, things that he hated, but this was perhaps the worst. He forced himself to slap Ross's face over and over, yelling as he did, until the eyes flickered open.

"Listen to me!" screamed Singleton. "Did you tell them? Did you tell them?"

The face, brilliant white in the lamp's beam, was already that of a corpse. Only the lips moved and then at first there was no sound.

When the words came they were only just audible. "I wanted to. I tried, but she wouldn't let me speak."

Then he died.

Singleton stared for a long time, almost drugged with horror. When it came, the noise so scraped his already raw nerves that he spun around almost before his mind registered it.

There was a man in the doorway, little more than a bulky shape against the light from the adjoining room. There was no mistaking the gun in his hand, though.

He moved closer, and Singleton made out some details of the man's face. He looked as though he might be an Arab.

Singleton still had his pistol in his hand. It pointed towards the floor, but nevertheless he felt sure that even if he were hit he would raise it and fire back.

The newcomer took another pace forward, and his eyes stared at Ross's body before focussing on Singleton. There was no mistaking the question they asked.

"The Mr Nobody of the hijack," said Singleton. "Some poor bastard called Ross. No good to them, so they tortured him to death."

"Why do you think they'd do that?"

"Fun? Practice? Who the hell knows. They're animals."

The man seemed satisfied. He nodded towards the doorway. "Let's get out of here," he said.

They moved into the room where the four drugged hostages still lay unconscious.

The stranger spoke again. "You're the American," he said. He began to laugh. "The bastards sold them to both sides, you *and* us."

"You're the Russian?" It was obvious, but Singleton had to ask.

Gozori's laugh became manic. "They brought us here at the same time," he said. "I imagine we've both paid them. Now they'd like us to kill each other." He stared at Singleton's gun. "We could, you know."

"Take your man," said Singleton wearily. "If that's all you want."

Gozori stared at the American for a long time. He recognised something in the man's voice and eyes, something he had long felt in himself – a terrible weariness. "That's all," he said quietly.

He hesitated, and Singleton realised that the Russian was reluctant to compromise his safety by lifting Volkov while he, Singleton, still held a gun.

"Why don't we both put our weapons down?" he said.

Gozori nodded and began to move his pistol towards his shoulder holster and then paused. Singleton watched the Russian's face and realised what he was thinking: if both men holstered their guns he would still be at a disadvantage if the American tried to draw while he was lifting Volkov.

"I'll place mine on the floor and kick it well away," he volunteered.

The Russian smiled and slowly began to holster his gun as Singleton bent and set his down and then with a push of his toe sent it sliding a good six feet away.

It took the Russian several minutes to get the deputy minister hoisted and on to his shoulders. His face was contorted with the effort, but Singleton stood back, not volunteering to help.

Gozori gave a final smile before he began stumbling slowly towards the doorway. He was about ten yards into the open when Singleton remembered about the thirty-minute warning – although he was not sure he would have said anything.

The first shot spun Gozori round, making him drop the body. The second propelled him backwards, and the burst that followed removed half his head.

A second burst raked the body of the deputy minister which, in its unconsciousness, did not even twitch.

Singleton, frozen on the floor, watched but did not move. To have done anything would have been pointless. The Russian and his minister were so obviously dead.

There was a back exit, through a window, and ten minutes later when the police arrived all they found were the surviving hostages and the bodies. Singleton had gone.

# 23

"Priceless. Literally beyond price," said Singleton.

They were standing in Muntwick's icon room. Two months had passed and Singleton's face was heavily bandaged.

He had had plastic surgery – reluctantly, because he had not been convinced that it was necessary. But Warren had been persuasive: if he did not plan to hide away in a new place or a new country, his face had been seen enough by both the terrorists' contacts and by people who might link him with the escape to constitute a danger.

Now Warren stood next to him. "You know you're officially dead," said Warren. "Even your wife and son think so."

Singleton shrugged. "I don't imagine you'll tell them." He himself had told one person – a two-line note, typed, with a token to prove it was from him: half of a pair of cufflinks she had once given him. Almost adolescently, he carried the other cufflink in his breast pocket.

Singleton led Warren to the next icon – he and Muntwick now spent a lot of time together in this room.

"I'm sorry about the messiness," said Warren. It was only the second time they had talked and the first had been brief and businesslike on a 'safe' phone link.

"I imagine you'd have killed Ross anyway," said Singleton. His voice hid the emotion he felt. On bad nights he awoke and wondered how long Ross would have taken to die.

It was then he most wanted Kate, just to hold him, help him back into sleep again. He hadn't given an address in his note; he doubted he would see her again.

Warren's voice interrupted his thoughts. "There's one other thing," said the CIA man.

"Yes."

"Tape worm. You made me give them to you."

Singleton waited, but he knew what was about to be said.

It was these pills that Singleton had persuaded the jailed terrorists to take in the belief they were protection against chemicals that would be used in the prison break.

"I'll tell you now, because it will be obvious soon," Warren continued quietly. "What I gave you were fakes. Sugar pills. Nothing." He spread his hands and waited for Singleton's reaction.

Singleton let out a faint laugh, and his voice was resigned. "They probably wouldn't have worked anyway," he said. "From what I remember hearing about the tests on animals, they sometimes passed straight through."

Warren was relieved at the tone. "I'm glad you understand, George," he said. "That you realise why I had to do it, that you accept there are rules even in this."

He knew immediately he should have kept quiet.

"Rules!" Singleton's voice echoed. "Rules with shit like that!"

Warren had to defend himself. "Look, there are things you do and things you don't do even with people like these. For God's sake, George, the politicians can do and say what they like, but we're going to have to live with these people. Just like we did with the Russians and even the Nazis way back before them, we're going to have to formulate some ground rules . . ."

He paused, turned. Singleton was already at the door.

"You formulate the rules, Cord," said Singleton. "Leave me be." He shrugged his shoulders, and began to laugh, a strange sight in his bandaged head. "I guess I knew what you'd done anyway."

They met just once more, months later.

Singleton was now called Pearson, and looked totally different – cosmetic surgery had shortened his nose, intricate dental work had altered the line of his jaw, electrolysis had removed hairs along his browline, heightening his forehead.

He now spent part of his time looking after Muntwick Jr when he went outside – but that was not often because all the boy wanted to do since the hijack was sit on the floor and recite nursery rhymes. All Singleton knew of the other two rescued hostages was what he had read: the Frenchman was back running his business as before but now travelled nowhere, it seemed, without bodyguards and elaborate security precautions. Of Jennifer North there were continuous reports. One, he recalled, was that she had not needed an operation after all. Another, soon after, announced that divorce number four was underway.

Warren had arranged this meeting with Singleton. He was on his way out as head of the CIA – and he knew it. But before he went, he wanted to know.

The first of the freed terrorists had died about four months after the escape. An Irishman called Michael O'Dare Flynn. The reports were sketchy, but apparently he had started to feel ill after about a month.

Nothing startling, of course. People did die.

But then there had been news of a second and third and fourth . . . all in different parts of the world, all spread over some months.

"What was it George?" asked Warren. "Frederick," said Singleton. "Not George – Frederick Pearson. Singleton's dead."

Then – "What was what?"

"What did you do to them?"

Singleton did not reply.

"You don't have to say anything," said Warren. "I guess I know. I checked it all out. The reports were pretty detailed, and all similar. We'd have looked at a body if that wouldn't have been too obvious."

Singleton still said nothing.

"You fed them something radioactive," said Warren. "Something that wouldn't do anything for a month or so, and then . . ."

He peered into Singleton's eyes, but still saw no reaction.

"Where did you get it, George?" Warren shrugged. "You don't even have to tell me. It was from Muntwick, wasn't it? Easy for him. The shipment to Spain's on record. No attempt to hide it. All done by the book. Even a doctor on hand to sign."

He paused before continuing. "I talked to our experts. We don't know *exactly* what it was, but they reckon an isotope giving off alpha rays – despite what everyone thinks they're not all that dangerous unless they're ingested. Fairly safe to pick up quickly. But did you sweat a bit, George, when you did it?

"Then they reckon it would need ideally to be an isotope chemically similar to calcium so that the body is deceived and deposits it in the bones. They would say radium. Are they right, George? Radium probably in food or drink, undetectable unless you'd got a Geiger counter. Then into the stomach and on to the bones where it starts destroying the bone marrow straight away . . .

"They stop making blood. Result – death. Without treatment, weeks. Even with – and none of these got it – a few months. Am I still right, George?"

Singleton shuddered and closed his eyes. He saw the child, her leg blown away. He could see Ross staked out on the wall, face contorted, body torn with holes, caked with drying blood.

He took Warren's arm and squeezed violently. "There are no rules, Cord," he said. "From now on, there are no rules . . ."

# 23

They killed him two Thursdays later at seven twenty-seven on a fine warm evening.

It was possible to be precise about the time because there were two eye-witnesses across the street and his watch shattered and stopped.

The car mounted the kerb as it screamed around the corner. The witnesses claimed that it was travelling at upwards of sixty miles an hour.

He was probably killed by the initial impact but if not certainly by the second.

The car was found within twenty-four hours. It had been stolen. There was never any question of it being a routine hit and run – they don't stop after the impact and reverse over the body.

The police were reluctantly impressed by the meticulous care with which the driver had cleaned the interior of the car – usually there was at least a smudged, if useless fingerprint, a fibre of clothing, traces of dirt from the man's feet. This time, nothing.

The money in his wallet was taken by the two policemen and the ambulance driver who were first on the scene, and it proved difficult to clear of blood.

Nevertheless, there was enough money found in the belt under his shirt to pay for the funeral. At the mortuary, they also unloosened his clenched right fist and found a cufflink, a wren against a silver background, of little intrinsic value. One theory was that it was a keepsake he had taken into his hand after the first blow in the seconds in which he must have known death was inevitable.

Because George Singleton was dead, they buried him as Frederick Pearson, the name on the few documents which he carried.

No one answered an appeal for relatives. The police surgeon noted signs of recent cosmetic surgery about the face, and the police files recorded the possibility of a gangland killing.

Warren felt bad afterwards that no one attended the funeral, but it would have been too risky. And what was the point?

Singleton had been a dead man from the moment they had had to tell him about the cipher in order to get him to take the mission.

Warren was never able to understand how a man who had volunteered there were no rules could ever imagine that he would be allowed to continue living with so great a secret.

*Newsweek* would never have mentioned the killing, and then eleven weeks later, if it had not been followed by three more which, rightly or wrongly, the Chicago newspapers began to link.

There had been rumbling warnings of a gangland fight over territories, news generally was slack and – at *Newsweek* – the cufflink with the house wren motif seized an editor's imagination.

Kate saw it on the way home to see her parents, a break she felt she desperately needed. If she had not been on an airplane she doubted she would have read it – it was not a magazine she normally saw.

There was a police photograph of the corpse, looking somewhat unreal. She did not recognise it, but she knew. The cufflink told her.

She had not known whether they would ever meet again. She had welcomed the message from him telling her that he was alive and not dead as the rest of the world thought. But as to seeing him . . . their relationship had never been like that. If they met, that was enough. Their relationships just happened.

But this.

She held the magazine until her knuckles grew white and her fingers distorted the pages and left indentations of sweat.

She held it until the aircraft landed and the passengers disembarked. Then she tossed it aside, never wanting to read it again.

It could not be left like that, though.

She made the call from the booths in the arrivals lounge.

They fetched him to the 'phone.

"Ralph Leger speaking. Who is this, please?"

"Ralph," she said, "do you remember me? Kate Galbraith."

There was a pause, and then. "Remember you?" incredulously. "God, sure I do. Where are you?"

"At the airport. I'm home." She drew a breath. "Ralph, can we meet? Soon? Now, if we can. I've got a story. And I think you'll want to hear it."